# WHISPERS OF GRAY
## KEEP IN THE LIGHT
### BOOK 2

DAVID MUSSER

Copyright (C) 2021 David Musser

Layout design and Copyright (C) 2024 by Next Chapter

Published 2024 by Next Chapter

Edited by Megan Anderson, proofreading by Tyler Colins

Cover art by Jaylord Bonnit

This book is a work of fiction. Names, characters, places, and incidents are the product of the author's imagination or are used fictitiously. Any resemblance to actual events, locales, or persons, living or dead, is purely coincidental.

All rights reserved. No part of this book may be reproduced or transmitted in any form or by any means, electronic or mechanical, including photocopying, recording, or by any information storage and retrieval system, without the author's permission.

Whispers of Gray is my second novella. I dedicate this to my parents. They passed several years ago. I can picture how proud of me my mother and father would be.

My mother got me interested in the horror genre. I remember watching Frankenstein, Dracula, or The Wolfman as a kid and being scared to sleep that night until I crawled into bed with my parents.

It was such a joy to return home from school or watch Dark Shadows with Mom in the afternoons on days when I did not skip school.

My father, to whom I talk every time I start up his 79 GMC Sierra, was not as much of a talker but a thinker. When I was a kid, he did not speak much, but what he said was valuable. One of the lessons he taught me was to be comfortable riding in silence, just enjoying each other's company.

# ACKNOWLEDGMENTS

This book was so much fun to write, and in doing so, I want to thank:

Megan Anderson - Again, I cannot thank you enough! I am writing this while the first book is very close to being completed in the editing process. Thank you for all you have done and all you are doing. I do hope everyone appreciates how much you have put into this. I know I do.

Rachel Musser - Maybe someday I will write you a funny story or a drama about life, but I am so thankful for all the support you show me when I am working on this. I enjoy talking to you about it when we are riding to the gym, and hearing how proud of me you are makes me so incredibly happy.

Lisa Musser - Thank you for being there for me. I remember the first time I saw you. It is a shame it took me another couple of months to say hello.

Finally you, the Reader, I am so happy with the feedback from my first book, and I hope that you keep enjoying my work. Please visit my website, www.dmusser.com, for ways to contact me or email feedback@dmusser.com.

# CONTENTS

Preface     vi

1. The Walk     1
2. Recovery     9
3. The Mansion     18
4. The Gym     25
5. The Stairs     32
6. Brother Paul     41
7. Homecoming     49
8. The Man in White     57
9. The Lake     63
10. Revelations     70
11. Angels and Demons     79

Afterword     86
From the Author     93
Music Playlist     95

# PREFACE

The man looked up, his hands folded on the metal desk. He saw the blood on his arms. The left forearm was bent at a very odd angle compared to the other. With a determined look, he grabbed his left hand with his right and pulled it; after a moment, there was a loud pop. "There, that's better," he said to the empty room.

He saw a wireless speaker on the desk that he knew must contain a microphone. The room was dark, lit only by two battery-powered lanterns, one on low as if he was going to sleep.

He stood up and walked around the room. Concentrating, he looked at and felt the walls with his hands. "There must be a weakness in this cage." His pants were torn as if they had been dragged through the bushes. He could feel the scratches on his legs and knew the ankle was broken. No, it's sprained.

The room was square, about twenty by twenty, and the ceiling was about twelve feet high. The remnants of dinner laid in the corner on the floor next to a metal rocker with a book on the seat. The rocker looked like someone had yanked off an old porch in the country. He looked down at the title of the book and laughed. "Fitting," he spat out to the empty room.

The room was completely enclosed. No obvious doors. The

man knew there was one, but it was some type of lever system. It could only be opened if another was closed. No way out.

Outside the room, the Man in White asked the technician beside him while the mic was muted, "When can we get visual? And are the other sensors online?"

"With a sealed metal box? It is all we can do right now to have this. We are working on it and hope to have something in the next few months. This is a---" The technician was cut off by the man in the cage, who had started to yell.

"Hello! Whoever you are, I want my lawyer!" he demanded, then in a lower, more controlled voice, " You know who I am. You know that I have friends all over the world, and you would not like them." Then, after another short pause, he started to scream again. "You have no right to hold me!" He picked up the wooden chair he had been sitting in and slammed it against the wall, shattering it.

"Who are you?" asked the Man in White over the microphone.

"Who are you?" he responded quickly and started to laugh before he added, "Names have power, don't they, my friend? We are that, are we not? How long have we been friends? I don't know why the cage. Your plan didn't work, so let me out. It is all OK now."

The Man in White frowned; he remembered his friend. Remembered the first time they met. He had been hunting shadows, but this man was troubled by something else.

"Is my girlfriend there? You should have a go with her. You would like her, very sexy," the man in the cage added as he cackled with laughter.

"Who are you? Name yourself; are you not proud of who you are? You have told me you have so many friends. Who are they, and why are they not here or looking for you?" he asked in a rush, unsure how to best communicate with him.

Sniffing, the man in the cage said, "Wait. One of my friends

## PREFACE

was here. I know it; one was here, and I could feel him. The stench of his death is all around."

The technician transcribing the conversation for later hands shook, and he backspaced a few times because of mistyped keys. He looked up at the Man in White and mouthed, "How does he know?"

"Was it one of the babies? Is that what you had? The young ones are so weak." Then sniffed again and said, "No-no, you did not. You killed the father." He picked up a blanket from the bed, laid it on the only other chair in the room, a metal rocking chair, and sat down.

He saw a book on a metal table, picked it up, skipped a few pages ahead of where someone had marked it. Where he, must have stopped reading; with a wicked grin, he folded one page and ripped it out. Then, he skipped a few more ahead, ripped out another, laughed, and continued the process as he crumpled all the pages, placed them in his mouth, and chewed slowly.

"I am sorry I threatened you. That was not very nice of me. You see, it has been a long time since I was in a cage, and never one as good as this. I was upset for a moment. No more threats," he said and then laughed again a wicked laugh.

"I am not threatening you because you are already dead. She is awake, and she is coming for you. I could tell you where she is if you want?" suggested the man in the cage, a question in his voice.

"Why would you do that?" the Man in White asked.

"Because if I am nice to you, maybe you will let me out. What do you say? I tell you where she is right now, and you let me out." Then, paused for dramatic effect, added, "But wait---I have a good idea, and this will be fun. I will tell you where she was this weekend, and you will know that I speak the truth. See if we have a deal," he finished.

Smiling at the speaker, he tasted the air, and they unconsciously leaned toward the speaker; he started the story off with,

# PREFACE

"There once was a boy named Gary who had puke on his shoes." Gary could not believe that someone had puked on his shoes.

What a crappy thing to do to someone. The water rushed by; he stood beside the creek and dipped his feet in one at a time. He did not care if his shoes got wet; they would dry quickly. He just wanted to get rid of the puke. He had pulled up his jeans. They were off-brand but new, and he did not want to get them wet.

He had swimming trunks for later if people wanted to swim in the creek. As he stood beside it after washing them, he felt the squishing in his shoes and wished he had just wiped them off. That was something to worry about later.

For now, he was on a quest. A quest to find a cave that he and his buddies, one of which had puked on his shoes, could explore. His father had told him of its location when Gary mentioned where the bonfire would be. It was a party, but Gary thought calling it a bonfire would make his father not think it was a drunken college party.

His father had told him to avoid the cave. But Gary's drunken mind decided for him, and he blurted out that there was a cave. How hope was to impress everyone and make them all like him more. Especially his ex-girlfriend.

Shoes cleaned, he walked on the path; he finally saw the way to the cave and stopped. The sounds of the night creatures were so loud here and so beautiful. He reached into his pocket and pulled out his phone to record some of the sound, hoping it would sound fantastic as a ringtone.

He continued down the path and stopped again. He listened, but nothing but a faint sound of the music over the other hill. The noise of the creek mostly drowned that out, and there were no more night creatures, no more frogs, no insects, nothing.

He turned around a couple of times and almost fell. Then, he stopped, turned back on the path, and walked ten steps before he heard the night creatures. It was not as loud as earlier, but he knew if he kept going, it would get louder. "Wow, I have drunk a lot," he said in slurred words. Gary figured it was just his imagi-

# PREFACE

nation and wanted to check out the cave so badly that he kept walking toward it.

Sweat broke out on his forehead. He brushed it away and looked around. Turned on his phone's flashlight. "Don't be a baby, Gary; it's your imagination." He made it to the mouth of the cave. Shining the light from his phone on the entrance, he saw it boarded up. The boards appeared to be ancient, with lots of space between them.

Gary grabbed one and pulled. It came off quickly, and he forgot that he was in danger. He forgot that there was no sound from the night creatures or insects. It took him a few minutes to clear the boards off the front of the cave. He stacked them all in a nice pile. "Maybe I'll do a bonfire here," he said. "Bring my ex back for a little fun," he continued with a laugh. Knowing that he didn't stand a chance with her anymore. They had dated when he was eleven; now, at nineteen, he had never quite gotten over her. If you hadn't guessed yet, Gary was a virgin.

He sat down at the mouth of the cave, bowed his head and said, "Why doesn't she like me?"

"I could tell you all the reasons if you are interested?" asked the man in the cage.

Gary turned his cell phone light off and leaned against the cave's outer wall. He flipped through the apps and started to play some candy game on it. His plan, if he had one, was to rest there for a few minutes and head back to his tent. His friends would be so happy that he found the cave; maybe she would be proud of him.

The light from the phone illuminated the cave, and patterns of light appeared between the shadows. Gary didn't notice the tendrils of darkness that reached out of the cave and surrounded his face; he didn't feel them on his legs as they traveled his pant legs. The shadows circled him, and they made sure not to touch him. They knew the life-draining power they had, and it was not yet his time. They wrapped around each other moved over his clothes, but never touched his skin. Gary, eyes locked on the game, never noticed them.

"I never win at this," he said to no one and then looked up freezing in place, as he noticed them. Something like this had happened to him once before; he had been swimming in the ocean. He swam as deep as he could, and when he resurfaced, he was surrounded by jellyfish. He'd found himself in the middle of them, knowing if he moved, he would be stung by all of them.

In the ocean, his bladder had let go into his swim trunks before they floated away. Seated on the ground in front of the cave, a wet spot appeared on his pants as his weak bladder had let go, as Gary finally realized the danger he was in.

The creatures appeared to not have noticed him wet himself and continued to circle around his legs; they curled under his chin, behind his ears. They are toying with me, Gary thought as his body shook uncontrollably.

"Gary did not know how right he was. For them, food that was terrified tasted so much better, and to them, he was only food," said the man in the cage before he continued.

Some of the shadows were as long as snakes, but some were as short as pencils and very thin. Kind of amazing; what are they? His mind wondered. For a second, he thought he saw one that looked like a spider as it crawled up his pants.

He saw one go under his hand and flipped on the phone's flashlight. The creatures stopped, and all of them scattered; they pulled back into the cave. The one he was shining the light on had appeared to be in pain or discomfort. Like an earthworm when you cut it in half, wiggling, he thought. He shone the light on it; he wanted to find its head. Gary noticed it no longer floated in the air as it first appeared. It was attached to the cuff of his shirt. The creature started to turn transparent as Gary held the light on it. It only took a few seconds before he could through it, and then the light, as if it was fire, burned entirely through, and the tiny shadow was gone.

"What the... ?" he said aloud. Gary stood up and proclaimed,

# PREFACE

"I don't know what that was, or they were, but I'm out of here." He started to get up, and planned was to run toward the path.

"His body sensed more danger, and while he should have run away, he turned toward the cave, holding his phone's flashlight before him like a cross to hold back the darkness. A cross might have held more power over the creature that came out of the cave. The smaller ones followed in its wake."

Gary screamed, and the creature wrapped itself around him; his screaming stopped with the touch of the creature; he no longer had control over his body as he was laid on the ground, arms spread wide.

His eyes were open. He noticed the colors starting to fade from his shirt as it dissolved. All of his clothes appeared to age and fade away to dust. Gary lay there. He tried to scream and move, but no sound or movement was possible. You see, his body was completely numb from her touch.

The shadow moved upward and blocked the moon's light that had appeared through the clouds as if it wanted to try and save him. The moon had little power over the leviathan-like creature, though. Her little shadow children started to move over Gary's body. He felt a sting like a jellyfish every place they touched, but he still couldn't scream or move. He was held powerless as the shadow spider-like creature crawled up his neck onto his face and into his open mouth as they explored his naked body.

Above him, the shadow in a voice unheard by human ears said, "My hungry children, feed and grow. Feel his fear and devour him." Gary noticed one of the smaller ones as it moved down his arms to his hands and fingers; he felt the sting and then nothing from his fingers. Watching, he saw the tips of his fingers fade one by one and then disappear before they turned to dust, the same as his clothing had. Inside his head, he screamed as the fingers on the other hand were devoured, as the tiny creatures fed on him. They moved up his hands, and several swirled around and around, so much faster than before until his hands were cut off at the wrists. There is no blood? It was the last sane thought Gary ever had. The children slowly devoured his extremities. The mother was proud of her children as they fed on Gary, fed on him body and soul.

"Gary had thoughts and dreams, pathetic as they were; he had them, and they devoured him just like they will devour you," the man in the cage finished. He crossed his arms behind his head, shut his eyes, and said, "She will kill you slowly. She enjoys that."

# CHAPTER 1
# THE WALK

The dog barked, and Jeff tried to wake up. Shaking his head several times to clear the dreams, he glanced at the clock. "1 a.m. ... f'n dog," he grumbled to himself. Luckily, his wife was still asleep. That was all he needed was for the dog to wake her up. She had taken a couple of sleeping pills earlier.

She had been having trouble sleeping since she started the new job. The hours were crazy for her, and he tried his best to help. Never should have got the dog, he thought as he got out of bed. Stopping at the rocking chair on his side of the bed, he quickly pulled on his pants.

Since the dog only barked once, he took his time. If it's not in a hurry, I'll be out there for a while, he thought as he grabbed a t-shirt from the top of the hamper, sniffed it, and pulled it on; he glanced back at his sleeping wife and thought to himself. She is so beautiful. If she did not have to be up early, I'd be rubbing her neck, kissing that spot she likes on her back!

He paused, walked back to the bed, and covered her feet. She had pulled the sheets up again in her sleep, and he knew she would wake up miserable if her feet were cold.

Walking down the hall, he was glad they were still crating

the puppy. He knew it would not be long before she was trained and, most likely, sleeping between them in the bed. Why had I told her I loved dogs when we first met? It was not exactly a lie. He had no opinion of them, but what type of monster didn't like dogs? So, Jeff said those three little words, "I love dogs," and they became man and wife a year later. He had just finished his degree; she was already a not-so-starving artist.

She would tell people she lucked into it, but he knew she had talent. She was an outstanding painter. Who knew you could make money painting? He often wondered, but that new car in the driveway was as much proof as anything.

This new job, though, was something he could not understand. Why someone would want to commission a portrait from 3:00 a.m. to 6:00 a.m. daily was beyond him. It was only supposed to be a three-week gig, but after several false starts, one of which was when her client tore up the canvas and threw it on the fire, she was inexplicably still working there. That incident had kind of freaked her out. The client had apologized, though, and the next day, a new car with a big blood-red bow on top of it was in the driveway.

Jeff's mind had been wandering, and he pushed his long hair back out of his eyes and scratched gently on the bald spot on top. Sarah said she couldn't see any hair loss, but he felt it. So, he scratched gently to make sure it did not cause any more premature hair loss. A part of him wondered why he had thought of the bow as blood-red.

He grabbed the leash, opened the cage, quickly grabbed the dog by the collar, and hooked it. "There you go, puppy. Damn. We have to give you a name soon. Who are you?" Jeff was still bent down, his face at her level, and he was rewarded with a lick to the nose.

She whined a little, so he stood up and went through all the training the pet store had told him. He inquired if she had to go pee, and then off they go. Love to put in a dog door, he thought, but knew that Sarah was paranoid of snakes and frogs and anything else that could sneak in, for that matter, so the idea was out of the question, for those reasons, sure, but mostly because their new puppy was a mastiff who within six months will weigh in at about 100 pounds and be almost her full height. I bet she will be able to touch my shoulders when standing on her hind legs. Excuse me. I would like a man-sized dog door, please, he laughed.

At the door, he pushed his feet into his sneakers and pressed the heels down. This created a makeshift pair of clogs. His wife called him lazy for doing this whenever she caught him, but he would shrug it off each time, telling her how comfortable it was and encouraging her to try it sometime. "So easy to put on or take off," even with his wonderful grin, she was not impressed, and he knew she would always think of him as a little lazy.

Looking up as he walked with the puppy, he hoped she would finish her business soon enough for him to get another hour or two of sleep. He didn't have to wake up with Sarah when she got ready to go, but he had always felt better if they kissed before either of them left for work. A silly tradition, but one that he hoped to continue until he passed away.

There was no question of who would die first. Genetics was not on his side. His father and grandfathers on both sides died young and balding. Jeff did what he could to prevent this. He worked out, stopped drinking, and tried to eat right. The keyword on that was tried.

Sarah's parents and grandparents were still alive and played hearts or one of those card games on a weekly basis.

The puppy kept walking around. She had circled the new car twice before she moved on to the small yard. She looked up at the streetlight and barked to let it know who was boss, then circled her favorite bush a couple of times, but nothing.

"Come on, pee," Jeff demanded, and the dog sat and looked up at him for a treat. He knew better than to talk to the dog when she was trying to pee. Now, it would be another twenty minutes before she was done; that was after she finally figured out Jeff hadn't said, "Sit."

Jeff was tempted to unhook the leash and just let her run around the yard, but he knew that with his luck, she would get hit by the only car that was driving in the subdivision. Who is driving in the subdivision this late anyway? He wondered. The vehicle had been driving up and down the few nearby streets for a while now; he had been tracking it in the back of his mind as they walked.

The car was some type of muscle car. Not on his street now, but the next one. He heard it first and then saw it as it passed between two houses. The puppy had heard it as well and barked at it to let it know who the boss was.

The funny thing was that when the dog barked, Jeff saw the brake lights hit for a second, almost as if the person in the car heard the bark and understood the implied threat. My imagination is working overtime, he thought.

He turned and pulled the leash a little, and the pup followed. Jeff walked it around the side of the house. It was new territory, he thought, and he hoped it would help her go.

Within a few minutes, it did. The puppy squatted, and when she was finished. Jeff praised her, and they headed back to the front of the house. "No playing," the trainer had said. "If you want to play outside with her, take her out again, but not when taking her to pee." Jeff thought this was bullshit, but he's never had a dog before, so he figured it would0 not hurt to do things by the book.

He stopped just after they had turned the corner. The puppy growled, and Jeff swallowed a couple of times in disbelief. The car was right in front of him. Still on the street but not pointed the way a car should be on the street, it faced them with the lights off. The engine had a gentle idle. "What the---" Jeff starts, and the puppy barks again and then whines, pressing its body against Jeff's leg. He felt a little bit of pee on the top of his foot and, for an instant, thought it was his bowels that let loose before he realized it was the puppy.

He shook his head in rage and disbelief and started to feel really pissed off after he saw how scared the puppy was. Jeff started to walk toward the car. The lights turned on then and temporarily blinded him; the engine revved up, and it became louder and louder. The mystery driver held the brake down, keeping the car in place while simultaneously pressing the gas pedal to the floor. The car tilted forward under the power. Jeff got madder. He knew they were going to wake up his wife if they kept this up.

He shielded his eyes partially with his free hand and could see the tires slowly start to spin as if the engine's power could not be held back much longer.

Jeff looked around for a weapon and saw nothing. The puppy growled again, louder this time, and Jeff was surprised as the lights went off. "Good girl," he whispered, not knowing whether she was responsible for the light going off, but her courage was enhancing his. She had not given up, and he felt like he should have reinforced that.

There was going to be a fight; this was going down. He took a deep breath and hooked the leash to a bush. No need to let the puppy get hurt if I have to jump quickly, he thought as he broke into a run toward the driver's side door.

He was a good thirty feet away but having always been fast, he cleared the first twenty quickly. He stared at the windshield, trying to see who was driving, as he cleared the next five feet. The car eerily remained in place, the sound of the revving engine continued to escalate crazily.

Just as he reached the street, the car surged forward. "Stupid, stupid," Jeff uttered aloud as the car came at him. How did you die? Well, I charged a car.

The distance between them closing fast, Jeff prepared to leap out of the way, but as the streetlight caught the driver's face, he was frozen in disbelief.

The car struck him; his legs went under the car, and both ankles shattered as the car pressed him forward. His head bounced off the hood, and he heard a loud crack and knew that his neck was broken. The rest he saw as his head tossed from side to side, up and down, with no control as the car continued to drive forward. Not the puppy, he thought as he realized for the first time in his life that he was a dog person.

He remembered how sweet she was when she licked him on the nose and smiled. The car stopped, and he heard the driver put it in reverse. Never could drive a clutch; he was glad to no longer feel anything. He was being dragged back through the grass---his shoe caught in the bumper. He wondered if it would drag him all the way to hell when the car jumped back over the curb, which caused his foot to slide out of his shoe, and he finally stopped moving.

The car did a quick U-turn and speed out of the subdivision.

Jeff thought for a second that it had just disappeared, but that must have been a trick of his eye.

Jeff laid in the grass. Not sure if he was bleeding. He could not feel anything, only able to blink his eyes and moan, but other than that, he could do no more than wait. He tried to call out, but his lungs were on fire, and he could not catch his breath.

He heard something rustling in the bushes and wondered what was going on when the puppy ran over to him and started to lick his face. "I love you too," he croaked.

The puppy continued to lick his face until he was awake and then curled up beside him. It seemed to Jeff that every time he started to go back to unconsciousness, she would lick his face.

He heard his wife as she called his name from inside. He was not sure if she had awoken from her alarm or something else had her searching for him before it was to wake her. Had it been a few hours or only a few minutes? It was so difficult to tell time. The puppy started to bark louder than he would have thought possible.

Sarah was awakened by the blaring alarm. Should never

have taken this commission, she thought All of her other work was done on her time in her studio, but this guy wanted her to paint him at such an odd hour. She's not allowed to take pictures of him so that she could paint at her home, and he dictated everything must be left at his home... or mansion if she was being honest. It had to be one of the largest homes in the valley, but he doesn't make a big thing of it. Having dismissively said, "My parents had money and took care of me. I do my best to give back, and one of my charities wanted a portrait." It was almost as an apology for having hired her.

He had explained that he was paranoid of his image being used online and as for the odd hours, he spent a lot of time online with his clients in Japan, so really for him, he is just getting off work at 3 a.m.

She reached over, feeling for Jeff, found only his cold side of the bed instead. She had a bad dream but other than that, had slept well. She had been having bad dreams lately. Maybe the puppy needed out, she thought as she called his name quietly "Jeff." Wondering where he was she got up and pulled on her robe.

"It's a mom robe, can we burn it?" Jeff asked when she had gotten it. She defended the choice, explained to him how comfy it was and how warm and that she could not go through life wearing something he'd picked out of one of those magazines or websites.

She grabbed her cell phone out of habit and put it in the front pocket.

She loved him so much but, in some ways, wished he would grow up. The puppy was more of a test of him than her desire for a dog. Is he ready to be a father? she often wondered. She had been thinking more and more about children lately and thought I rock this mom robe.

In the kitchen, she saw his shoes were gone and opens the door "Jeff, you out here?"

She heard the barking and the sound of distress and was

running outside without her shoes on. When she saw him, she quickly dialed 911. She reached him, looked down to see his eyes were wide open. The puppy was curled around him, it had been licking the tears and blood off of his face.

She leaned over him to tell him it would be OK, and is greeted with Jeff's scream in her face as he saw the face from the car again. Sarah could not understand and somewhere in his brain, Jeff knew that it couldn't have been Sarah driving but that realization would come later; for now, he screamed and the puppy growls.

## CHAPTER 2
## RECOVERY

Jeff woke in the hospital. He could smell the antiseptic and heard the hum and beeping of the equipment in the room. He focused on opening his eyes, but they were slow to respond. *Ha! I was run over by a car, and I still cannot get that song out of my head.* "Click, click, boom," he said aloud before finally opening his eyes. The lights were so bright he had to squint.

"What was that?" the nurse asked.

"I can talk?" he asked hoarsely.

"Well, of course, you can; you're dead," she said calmly.

Jeff looked at her and saw Sarah in a nurse's outfit. Her long blond hair was pulled back. Her features were striking against the tight outfit.

Jeff screamed and woke up. The room was dark. *Just a dream, thank goodness. I hurt all over,* he thought, then smiled. "I hurt," he said aloud. He knew that if there was pain, he was feeling. He could feel a tube near or in his nose and thought it must be oxygen.

Jeff looked around the room; there was a light in the hall. The door was open, and he could hear the nurses and doctors talking about different patients. Maybe even him.

"Lucky ... car drove on the grass ... it was soft ... and he sunk down some. His wife will be back... had to check ..." Different voices talked as they faded in and out before everything went completely dark.

Jeff opened his eyes and realized the pain was less. He was happy he could still feel. The light was on in the room; a doctor stood at the foot of the bed; he had been talking to his wife. They did not realize he was awake.

Jeff saw the doctor's look at his wife and instantly hated him. *Married above my league,* he thought.

"He will be in and out for the next couple of days. We are past the critical mark. He may never---" The doctor stopped when he saw Jeff's eyes were open. "Oh, great, you are with us," the doctor said and motioned for a nurse before going through the standard checks that Jeff figured, by the doctor's practiced touch, he must do a hundred times a day.

He told Jeff about his injuries and tried to give him hope for recovery. The doctor warned him that it would take a while and that he should not be in a rush.

*Click, click, boom,* Jeff thought, and started to hum the song in his head. He was not trying to be impolite; he just did not want to hear this. He figured that this emergency room doctor knew his stuff but doubted that anything would be sure until he visited a lot of experts. "What a mess." Jeff nodded at the appropriate points and thanked the doctor.

Sarah was holding his hand, and he could feel it. He even moved his fingers to brush her hand. It was not much, but it made him and her feel good. The doctor and nurse finished their process and left them alone in the room.

"Angel?" Jeff asked.

"Angel?" Sarah asked back, not knowing what he was talking about.

"Sorry, thought we had this conversation. That's her name. The puppy's name is Angel."

"How did you come by that?" Sarah squeezed his hand

lovingly, thinking about the name, already knowing that it was perfect.

"She told me ---" he started, and then time passed.

"Well, how are you doing today, Mr.---" the nurse started to say, then looked at
the chart.

Jeff knew she had not seen him before. "Please call me Jeff," he said a little less
hoarsely than before.

"Wonderful, I'm Alex. I will be with you for a lot of your recovery. You may hate me at times, Jeff, but I promise if you listen to me, I will help get you back as far as you can go."

He could no longer remember how many surgeries there had been. He was just glad they were over. *I just want to go home*, he thought, and then realized what she said; he blinked. This was the first person who had told him not what he wanted to hear but the truth. "As far as you can go?" he repeated and smiled at her.

"I find it best to not lie or obscure the truth. You have been here for ..." I looked at your chart and talked to your doctors. She told him about his different surgeries. "I'm private, so not with the hospital, but they have agreed to let me use their facilities." She then went on to explain the process and gave him some "toys," as she called them, to work on his hand strength and also to just give him something to do.

"There is a lot of hardware in you, and everything seems to be healing nicely. We will start tomorrow. I just wanted to let you know and meet you," she finished, standing up.

"Alex," Jeff called when she was at the door. As she turned, for a second, he saw his wife's face before he realized it was just a trick of the light and his imagination. She had long dark hair held in one of those French braids.

"Yes?"

"I'm sorry, but I cannot work out tomorrow. I did not pack any sweatpants," he said and laughed.

She smiled and winked at him. "Laugh it up now, big boy; tomorrow, you are mine."

Sarah came in as Alex was leaving, and they smiled at each other and said the standard greetings. He could already tell that they would be friends.

Sarah smiled and reached out for his hand. "You are going to be so happy,"

Jeff did not say anything. He waited and finally smiled, "With? Don't hold out on me, darling. I am going stir-crazy in this place."

Sarah smiled; this was the first time he had shown any real emotions. Almost as if he'd zoned out on the other visits. "You may not remember, but you wanted Angel to be trained as a service dog. In case… well, just in case, and I tried but none of the regular places would take her. Evidently, a Mastiff is not a good service dog. I think they are being silly, but it had to do with her not being able to lay under the seat on a plane and some other stuff. You would think that she could be trained." Her nose scrunched up in the smile at her own joke; Jeff loved her so much and nodded for her to continue.

"Anyway, Officer Morgan talked to a friend---" She stopped when Jeff looked at her questioningly. She told him how Officer Morgan had been around and talked to Jeff several times about the accident. She reminded him that his short-term memory had been impacted but was somewhat better. The officer was one of the first at the house and had really taken an interest in finding the driver.

*Sure, and you having long, beautiful blonde hair has nothing to do with it,* he caught himself thinking and then shook his head, only saying out loud, "I remember now."

She continued, "She is being trained by someone who used to train police dogs. The guy is a little odd but a good guy, I'm told. He will train her to help with security and, in general, be the perfect service dog for you."

"But aren't there rules?" he asked.

"She will not be a service dog but more of a guard dog, and with the way she growled at me when you were hurt, she is a natural. Maybe even an attack dog."

Jeff remembered this. He also remembered having a conversation with Angel that night. They talked about more than just her name. He just wished he could remember more. Not sure why, he kept what he did remember and the identity of the driver to himself.

"That is great!" he said, smiling. "Met with the therapist a minute ago. She said I'll be up and around in no time," he lied. He did not want to worry Sarah any more than he had already. These past months had been rough on her. Especially with him not being able to remember the previous visits.

Jeff started therapy the following day, and the next few weeks went in a blur. He works as hard as he can, but it was almost as if he was learning to move again. They had moved him when he was unconscious, Alex had explained. "To keep you from getting bedsores and other issues developing when you cannot move yourself."

"Small wins," Alex said often. "Focus on the small wins. Can I move my toes? Can I move my ankles, knees, hips, chest, arms, hands, fingers? And we have already seen you look at women walking by, so your neck works."

"I don't," he started to declare and realized, by the smile on her face, that she was joking with him. "Yes, small wins."

The therapy lasted a long time, and Sarah never once mentioned anything about money or life outside of the hospital. If Jeff had not been so focused on his recovery, he would have thought to ask. In the end, he could not walk or stand without help, but he was able to help Sarah lift him out of the bed. He used a handle mounted above the bed. It was a small win, but something.

The night before he was to come home, he got a cold chill and was about to call for a nurse for an extra blanket when he noticed a tall man standing in the doorway. He could tell right away that the man was not a doctor. *The suit is too classy ... or classic, is that the right word?*

"I'm Paul." the man said as if that was supposed to explain everything. Seeing the questioning look in Jeff's eyes, Paul continued, "I hired your wife before your accident." Then smiled, after he saw recognition in Jeff's eyes.

"I was sorry to hear about your office," Paul said and again saw the same questioning look. "Oh, you do not know. It is not my place to say. I am sorry. I should go."

Jeff stopped the man as he turned to leave. He knew this man had information he needed to know, and it turned out that he did. Jeff's company had been purchased and liquidated. There'd been some shady business practices going on. While the insurance would cover his medical bills, there was no unemployment insurance. He may be able to get social security, but that will take a while.

"She didn't tell me," Jeff said with a sigh.

"Well, I'm glad I came to talk to you. I have too much room in my house and if your wife stayed there ... and you, of course ... she could work on the portrait during the day. I know that this seems like an odd request, but with my hours, it would be nice to have people in the house."

Jeff could not believe what he was hearing. "I don't know. I wouldn't want to burden you. I thought she would've been finished by now," was the only thing he could think to say.

"That's my fault. I am very picky, and we have had to restart several times. That, and we put things on hold for a while. As far as being a burden, it's nonsense. I have been told that before your last job, you were a builder or handyman; is that the right term? And when you mend, as you can, do things you do. I have rooms that I do not think anyone has been in for a very long time. If I forgot to mention it, I have already built a rehabilitation room to Alex's specifications. I hired her to be your therapist. I did not tell Sarah, but I wanted to help. Please say yes. I would have taken this to Sarah directly, but I know that your mental state must be fragile right now."

Jeff couldn't believe what he had heard. *Did this guy just call him fragile?*

"Please don't misunderstand. I mean that as an explanation. Think of it this way: if she had proposed this and wanted it, how would you have felt? Now, it is simply your choice. Bring it up to her or not. If you do not, I give my word that I never will."

Jeff shook his head in disbelief, and realized that this man was offering him a lifeline; with his job being gone, the bills must piled up. They had savings, but Sarah must have been forced to dip into them by now. They were saving for a house so they could stop renting, and now look where they were. He wondered how much she had borrowed from her parents as well.

"I will talk to her ... and thank you. I mean that. Thank you! I guess you are right about my mental state. I seem to be having lots of memory flashes and ..." He trails off as something in Paul's eyes, just for a second, gave him an odd feeling.

Paul broke the spell when he clapped his hands together and said, "I am so glad. This is perfect. I will notify the staff at my house to be expecting you. I am up some days but mostly at night. My father taught me you have to work when your customers are working or expecting you to."

Jeff liked him. He had not asked Sarah too many questions about him before. He trusted her, and he had a wonderful feeling about this. "Besides, what's the worst that could happen? Someone could run me over again?" he joked and though it turned out to be much funnier in his head, Paul was a good sport.

He gave his million-dollar smile and shook Jeff's hand. "I will not mention this to her. You talk to her and let me know."

"Oh, we have a dog ..." Jeff trailed off as Paul let go of his hand.

"I know, and I'm glad to say that I love dogs."

Jeff was sure of a lot of things in life, and he knew that Paul was a predator, maybe in business or life, and while Jeff liked him, he could sense that this was a lie. It would be like a fox saying, "I love dogs."

Sarah was not sure at first, but Jeff convinced her; he explained that his rehab would take a while yet and that he would be able to keep Alex. They could work together in his own private facility---Jeff really sold it. That last bit Paul had added on his way out the door. He told Jeff that his company required him to get regular checkups, and he found it easier to just have a nurse on staff. "She lives in one of the houses on the property," Jeff told Sarah.

"That is funny. I have never seen anyone but him," Sarah said, "but since he is a dog lover, he cannot be all bad."

The next day, Jeff was wheeled to the entrance. His insurance offered to pay for a motorized wheelchair since he's still not able to walk yet, but Alex refused it for him. Alex talked to the "boss," Sarah, and informed her that it would be better for his recovery if he worked for it.

"Do not make it easy on him. If he has physical problems, he cannot recover from, I would be the first to suggest a motorized chair, but that is not the case. Also, please do not feel sorry for him. You can feel bad that something happened, and you can help, but feeling sorry and just doing everything for him, including things he should do for himself will make his recovery take longer," Alex told her. Sarah knew she was right, and she had been feeling sorry for him.

It took a little bit for Jeff to get situated in the car. "A limo?" Jeff asked while getting in.

"Paul said for us to use it, said you would be more comfortable in something larger."

Jeff looked around and just had time to wonder where the driver was when the driver's side door in the back opened, and a giant, slobbering monster got in. "In you go, Angel," the driver said, and Jeff could believe it. Sarah had shown him pictures on her phone, but they had not done her size justice.

Angel looked at Jeff in the seat, his seatbelt on. He could hold himself upright, but if the car stopped, his legs still would not help him much. She looked at him, "chuffs." She was standing on the leather seat beside him and started to lick his face. Jeff knew that this breed slobbered, and he could feel it going down his shirt. Before the accident, he would have been grossed out; now, he simply loved her.

Jeff wrapped his arms around her neck and could feel the muscles underneath ripple as she laid down. She put her paws on his legs as he buried his face in her neck.

Sarah did not say anything. She was seated on the opposite seat facing him. Tears of joy ran down her face. She's wondered so many times if he was a good man, the right man for her. If he would be a good protector and a good father, and seeing the tears streaming down his face, she knew she had made the right decision. If only she could stop having nightmares that it was *her* driving the car.

# CHAPTER 3
## THE MANSION

Jeff was surprised to learn from Sarah that Paul could not meet them until later the next night. "He is traveling, so we will have the main house to ourselves for a day or so," she said brightly.

"How does he handle working nothing but nights?" he asked rhetorically, surprised when the driver responded, "Not very well. He tells me that it seems like it has been a thousand years since he saw the sun," he said with a laugh.

The estate was just a few miles outside the city. The driver turned out to be a great tour guide. "The lake is spring-fed, and the dock is wonderful. When you move again, you can swim in the lake or lie on the dock and relax. I don't know if your dog swims, but if she does, she will love it. If not, I'm sure she will love chasing the ducks."

Angel's ears perk up at the mention of ducks. Jeff covered her ears. "Think she heard you."

"Ha, that's great! She will love it. There are four smaller homes outside of the main house. I live in the one with all the cars out front. Go figure, right? Alex has the one to the right of mine." The driver kept talking and explained the layout of the property. He did not go into much detail about the main house.

He revealed he had only been in it once to help move in some of the weight equipment for Jeff.

"Sarah, it is hard to believe he is letting us move in. I really wish you would have told me how bad we were doing," Jeff said, not thinking about the driver listening at all, but he needed to say this now before forgetting.

"It is OK, and things will work out. It is very nice of him, and once you recover, you can help with some of the renovations he is talking about. He lets them know that the house was built in the early 1800s," Sarah told him.

The rest of the drive was relaxing. Jeff petted Angel; she was happy to have her with him again. *Let that car come for me again, and she will protect me,* he thought and was surprised to see Angel look up at him just then.

The car pulled up to the main house, and Jeff could not believe how huge it was. It was the largest house he had ever seen. It must have at least twenty or thirty rooms in it. Three floors above ground, and he'd already been told about the basement below, where the rehab center was ready for him.

A new ramp had been installed so that Sarah would be able to push Jeff up the ramp and into their temporary home. Angel hurriedly did her business outside behind some bushes before she charged into the house in front of them when Sarah opened the door.

Jeff laughed, "How much does she weigh now?"

"It's not polite to ask a girl her weight, but I promise you it is all muscle," Sarah responded, laughing as well. The rest of the afternoon was filled with unpacking and getting to know the house. They were on the ground floor. An elevator had access to all three upper floors and the basement, but Paul had asked that they stay on the ground level or basement.

"He has dog-proofed these levels, so if she destroys anything accidentally, or even on purpose, we are not to be too mean to her," Sarah said; she smiled at Jeff while he sat in the wheelchair beside the bed, deep in his own thoughts.

On his side, there was a chain so that he could pull himself up. They had a private bath with rails. His arms were more muscular now than they had ever been, so unless he had a spasm, he should be self-sufficient, and that made him very happy.

Sarah would never think of him as a burden, but he doesn't want things to be hard for her. Any harder than they already are. *Thank God, it wasn't worse,* he thought. Then, the song "Click Click Boom" started to play in his head again.

He could tell that Sarah was a little overwhelmed by the move and everything. "Tell you what. Let me get to know Angel a bit. I will take her outside and work on the control words you taught me. Maybe check out the dock---" He stopped upon seeing Sarah frown.

"Do not worry. I will not try to swim, and I will stay a safe distance back. I have my cell if there is an emergency, OK? Now, give me a kiss, and please, darling, take a nap. You have tonight off, so it will be good for you to relax a bit, and we'll finally get to spend a night together alone." He was interrupted by Angel's chuff and corrects himself. "The three of us can spend the night together alone."

Sarah kissed him, and as always, his toes curled a little at her touch. He had been wondering if that would happen now with the limited mobility and was glad when it did.

Turning in his chair, he started to roll himself down the hall, and he cursed Alex for not wanting him to have the motorized chair. Angel had a leash, but it was not on. He smiled to himself and held out the leash. Angel looked at it, and knowing his plan, she turned and headed for the door. "You too? Come back; it will be like a chariot race," Jeff called, putting his arms back to work the wheels.

She was waiting at the door for him, and he was glad that Paul installed the button to open the door. "This guy did a ton for me. For us. I have to find a way to repay him someday," he told Angel.

Outside, Jeff wheeled down the ramp; the paved drive was easy to navigate, and it did not take him long to get on the path to the lake. Jeff looked at the pavement and path and studied them for a second. He *did not pave this for me, did he?* Jeff found himself a nice shade tree, Then wheeling himself under, called "Angel," she instantly came to him.

He pet her and leaned down to let her lick his hands and face again. He called her to attention and went through the training routine that the trainer had given Sarah, who in turn had given to him.

"She is a smart dog. That is not always great because sometimes they may be smarter than you, the human. So, do not abuse the power she is letting you have as her alpha," the trainer had told Sarah.

"You are such a good girl," Jeff told her after a while and gave her another treat. Then figured she could use a nap as well. He called her to his side, and after she sat and laid down, he gave her the commands to relax and started to gently pet her head. He shut his eyes and hoped to have a wonderful daydream.

Sarah was looking out the window. She watched Jeff with Angel. She was so she started to cry, and had to brush them out of her eyes. There had been so much stress, and she never would have asked Paul for help, but she was glad that he offered.

*Go to sleep,* she thought to herself, but realized that she was doing anything she could to stay awake. Ever since the night of the accident, she's found it very hard to sleep. She'd been having bad dreams before, but that one scared her so much. "I should talk to Jeff," she said to the empty room. Then, she saw Jeff and Angel taking a nap and decided to try that herself.

*Please, no bad dreams,* she thought to herself. Jeff had told her a couple of days after the accident all about the car. How it had gone down a few streets first *almost hunting for you,* she thought, but had kept it to herself.

Then, when he came back around front, the car sat facing them, playing his own game of chicken with the car, he'd ran for the driver's side door. She could see him in her dream running for her. She had bit her lip and could still taste the blood and the desire to floor it. Then, just before she did, their eyes locked, and she knew that he had seen her. "I should ask him," she said to her pillow and then drifted off into an unrestful nap.

Jeff had the same memory as he slept. He remembered the car, the driver, and Angel after she had talked to him. She had said something else besides her name, but he couldn't remember what. In his dream, he did remember, and perhaps he would have remembered this time when he woke up, but other forces took over.

Jeff felt the wind blowing back his hair. It started to blow faster, and he could feel it on his face, so fast. He felt it on his chest and legs and was so glad. At first, it felt so good, almost like flying. He opened his eyes when he heard Angel barking behind him. Further back than she should have been. Then, a powerful growl came from her, so powerful that the earth seemed to shake.

Jeff opened his eyes, still partly asleep, and he realized that the wheelchair was moving. It was moving very fast. It was almost as if it had flown from the path to the dock. He looked back and saw Angel running after him, and for a moment, he could swear that he saw Sarah pushing him. She stopped, just let go of his chair, turned, and raised her arms up to protect herself as Angel burst through the vanishing image of Sarah.

Jeff, barely able to think, applied the hand brake slowly. Not wanting to have it stop at once. It would surely dump him face-first onto the dock or headlong into the lake. The chair slowed and slowed some more until he finally did not have a choice but to apply the brake fully. He stopped it with just a foot to spare. The chair and Jeff were on the larger portion of the dock, which ended in a large square that was meant for laying out or diving off.

Angel, behind him, faced the other way and continued with a low growl. Jeff turned the chair, and though he could not see anything, he knew that something was there. Something hunted him.

He pushed the chair toward the shore, and he uttered one word, "*Bewachen*." The German word for a guard. He had not known that they trained some dogs in German. He figured that she would be on guard anyway, but reinforcing the command was not a bad idea. They made it to shore and started down the path. Angel moved beside him, and the hackles on the back of her neck slowly eased down the closer they got to the house. He put his hand down to her, and she licked it.

"Danger gone now, girl?"

Angel responded with a single bark and a slobbery lick, and she wiggled her head under his hand to get him to pet her. "Good girl," he told her and gently stroked her hair while looking around. "OK. I do not think we dreamed that, girl. Unless I'm losing my mind."

He wheeled himself back to the tree, continued to pet her, and finally released her from her guard. He got out a brush that Sarah had put into his bag and started to brush her, using it to calm himself down. Her hair was short, but she seemed to like how the scratching of the brush felt.

"OK, girl, this is twice someone or something that looks like my wife has tried to kill me. I think if it is all the same to you, we keep it to ourselves for now. I may be going insane," he said finally and put his face down to her level.

Her response was affirmative. Or at least if that was what a dog licking your face meant. Sarah, covered in sweat, woke up. She ran to the window, expecting to see Jeff in the lake and Angel coming for her in revenge, but breathed a sigh of relief when she saw him brushing her.

"I knew he was a good one when he said he loved dogs," she said to the room. *What is wrong with me? I think I am losing it.*

Jeff looked up from his face bath and saw Sarah in the window. He gave her a friendly wave and motioned for her to join them. She declined but smiled at them and went to take a shower before he came back in.

Paul sat in his rocking chair by the window. Looked down on what just happened. The light felt good on his face as he rocked; his eyes looked down at the floor now, and his breath escaped in a sigh of relief. "Should get a dog."

"Can I help them?" he asked rhetorically.

Alex responded, "You have to try. What happened was not your fault, but you have to try and save them."

## CHAPTER 4
## THE GYM

"Dinner was great!" Jeff told Sara as she walked beside his wheelchair. Not pushing him. This was one of Alex's rules. "Do not do for him without him asking," she had said.

Alex explained that when people see someone in a wheelchair or with another disability, they immediately want to do something to help. The person with the disability just wanted to do what they needed to and get on with their business. "He will ask for help. I promise. Especially after training."

"Alex wants you at 8 a.m. tomorrow; are you ready?" Sarah asked.

Jeff looked up at her, not sure if he should say anything about before. Then Angel let out a little grunt. *Sometimes you are reading my mind,* he thought, and Angel yawned, slobber dripped out of her mouth. "Don't shake your head," Jeff said to her. "This is a nice house; they do not need slobber on the ceiling. Honey, hand me a towel. Yes, I think I'm ready. I doubt if she can be harder on me than she already was in the hospital. I think I must have pissed her off in another life," he laughed and could swear she grinned at him.

Upstairs in his office, Paul laughed. He sat in front of several computer monitors. They were installed years ago when his sister came to live with him under similar circumstances. "Did he piss you off in another life Alex?" Alex sat on his rocking chair, marked the page, looked up briefly, and flipped him off.

Jeff asked Sarah to push him, "I want to pet Angel," as they walked. Sarah was so happy they were getting close. She'd worried if he really liked dogs. *Some people lie about liking dogs.* In the bedroom, Jeff was able to get into the bed and under the covers almost by himself. He could have done it, but he knew Sarah needed to help as much as he wanted to feel her beside him.

He lay on the bed, then looked down, and Angel looked up at him very oddly. She moved her head to the left, then the right. "What's up with her?"

"You are in her spot," Sarah laughed.

Jeff frowned. "Is the bed big enough? And low enough for her?" In response, Angel answered him with a soft bark.

"Well, you have your answer," Sarah laughed, turned on her side to face him. "Good night, you two. Work it out. I love you both."

"I love you," Jeff responded automatically and then patted his hand on the side of the bed. "Come on, girl."

Sarah had been prepared because Angel slept beside her for a while. Sometimes, it seemed to her that she kept the dreams away, but not always. She found no reason to warn Jeff of what was going to happen. He was the one who had said, "If we get a dog ... I want a big one, a Mastiff."

The bed shook, and she heard Jeff grunt. She immediately opened her eyes to check on him. He was laughing and OK. "Wow, she weighs a ton," he said in between bouts of laughter, which Angel responded to with a couple of barks of protest.

Sarah and Jeff held hands, and Angel laid her head on top of their hands. They both felt the slobber but ignored it. She was a good dog. Looking at the monitors, Alex asked, "Think we will have any activity tonight?"

"I don't think so. It was out today, so that had to take energy from it. I wish I knew more, but so far, I'm only guessing. If you remember, after the accident, it was several weeks before there was any activity."

"How did the dog chase it away?" Alex asked while seated on Paul's chair.

Paul had gone to stand by the window. He had been looking out at the lake. "In some cultures, dogs have been known to ward off evil spirits. I also have an idea about iron. You always hear in the old folklore that iron and salt chase spirits away or at least keep them from entering a room or home. I am not saying this is a spirit vs telekinesis or some type of mental parasite, but I took the liberty of purchasing them a new collar. The leather was soaked in salt water for several weeks, and the studs all have iron cores that are silver-plated. Figure may as well try silver too," he said, then moved over to his rocking chair.

"You know this was her chair, my sister's. My parents got it when I was born, rocked me every night, and then rocked her. She had planned to rock her babies. Fuck. I need a drink," he said, got up, and went to the door.

"Get something to eat. Be quiet. Remember: you are still out of town. When you get back, I will get some sleep. Got to put Jeff through his paces tomorrow," Alex said absentmindedly, her eyes watching the monitors. She could not believe it, but she felt that the dog was watching her as well.

Thankfully, Jeff did not dream that night. He wasn't sure how he would have with Angel snoring the way she did. He smiled and stroked her hair when he woke up. She licked his fingers. Sarah was still asleep, so he got out of the bed as quietly as he could.

"Come on," he said, and Angel leapt from the bed.

Sarah woke briefly, smiled at them, and covered her head back up. She was asleep before Jeff was out of the room. Angel leads the way outside. The birds sang, and a couple of geese landed near the pond, so Jeff let Angel play. To get rid of some of that energy.

He figured they were alone and was surprised when Alex said, "Good morning," as if she suddenly appeared beside him.

"Wow, you are quiet," he said and laughed nervously. Not sure why she still made him nervous. There's something with this house. A feeling of being watched.

"I did not want you running away from me," She laughed, smiling at him. "Get something to eat, and I'll meet you downstairs in forty-five minutes. I'm going to get a workout in first."

Jeff smiled and wondered what she had planned for him. Angel taken care of a little breakfast for him, and then he headed for the elevator. There was a sign on it. "Out of order for Jeff. Use stairs."

"Fuck this," Jeff said and then looked around guiltily. She knew that he could not walk yet, much less use stairs. Then, he remembered that Paul was paying for this, and he needed to walk again, he opened the door to the basement. Surprised, he saw a chairlift and rails. A note with a little smiley face read, "Use chair lift today, but soon you walk, and your chair will ride."

At the bottom of the stairs, Jeff looked around as Angel ran over to greet Alex. "Sorry for the notes, but I wanted to piss you off. You need something to work towards, and everything we do will be with little goals in mind. We will also have some major goals. Our first major goal is the stairs. You will get to a point where your chair rides, and you make it down. Walking, crawling, sliding whatever you need to do, but you will make it. Then, later, it will be easier, and you will keep getting stronger. Makes sense?" Alex finished with the question.

"Yes, makes sense."

The basement was a good sixty feet by sixty feet. Paul turned this space into a mini gym and rehabilitation center. Jeff could not think of anything that he previously used in the megaplex gym he used to visit before the accident that Paul did not have there. He has all the free weights and some of the machines that would help him isolate specific muscles.

Alex pointed out the dressing rooms. "Yes, a His and Hers," she laughed

"Paul goes all out for people he cares about," she said and then looked away. She did not want to give away too much information. She finished the grand tour and showed him how the basement's entrance opened to an outdoor pool, a whirlpool tub, and a sauna.

She surprised him by pushing him around in the chair the entire time. He allowed her to do it, and Angel followed. Eventually, she figured out they were going to be there a while; she found a spot where she could keep an eye on him, did a few circles, and lay down.

"First, we start with naked squats," Alex said, smiling, and Jeff blushed.

"Naked what?"

She laughed some more. "Sorry, that is just a term to see if you can lift your own body weight or not. Did not mean to worry you."

Alex directed him to an area where there were a couple of cables within arm's reach. "Set the brake, and then reach up and pull yourself up. You have done this before, so this is what you are already doing. Now, lower yourself down slowly. Not by your arms, but by your legs. Let's see what you got. Think of it as a negative exercise."

Jeff shook his head in understanding, pulled himself up, and then tried to lower himself slowly. He made it about three inches before having to pull back on the cables.

"Good. Do it again," Alex barked like a drill instructor, and Jeff obeyed.

They did several sets of this and then moved on to other equipment. All the time she pushed him between the machines. Jeff could not believe how fast the time went, and when he looked up, and it was lunchtime already.

Alex pushed him towards the stairs, her voice more gentle than during the training. "How do you feel?" Angel noticed the change in direction, stood, shook, and followed.

"Good, bad. I'm beat," he responded in a rush to get the air out, then added, "Can I ask why you push me around down here but tell Sarah not to push me?"

"Yes, you may ask. If you give me one hundred and ten percent, I can and will help you get from station to station. If you goof off or don't give me what I know you are capable of, I will take the chair away and make you crawl between them," she said flatly.

The chair lift started up, and Jeff called down to her. "I'll hate you. Nothing personal, you understand, just saying," and they both smiled. Both knew how true it would be.

Sarah woke up when Jeff got back to the room. *Thankfully, no nightmares,* she thought. Got out of bed and kissed him. "Thank you for letting me sleep. Angel been out?"

On the word "out", Angel barked twice.

"Guess not. You get a shower. I will take her out. Do you need help?"

Jeff thought about this. Did he? "I do not think I do, but in any case, I will leave the door unlocked."

Paul had configured the shower so that Jeff could easily transfer from his wheelchair to the chair in the shower. "And this guy needs me for a handyman?" he said to himself, whistling. "Whoever he has did a great job," he finished, getting into the shower and turning it on as hot as he could stand.

After a while, he closed his eyes, and he could see Angel running outside; he saw Sarah, who stood there watching her and laughing while Angel chased a goose, then barked in frustration as it flew away.

He saw this the same as he could see the shower, almost as if the images both played out in his mind. He saw Sarah look at him, and when she smiled, her teeth were not the nice white teeth of his wife. They were sharp and jagged and vicious.

Sarah called to him. "You OK in there?" He awoke from his dream.

"Yes, I'm great; a seated shower is kind of cool. I took a nap," he laughed, but it turned into a frown when Sarah opened the door, concern on her face.

"Please don't do that, Jeff. I would be lost if something happened to you again." She hugged him so hard while the shower was still on that it got the back of her hair and shirt wet, but she did not care. "I love you," she told him, and Jeff felt so good.

Jeff smiled at her soaked shirt; she kissed him on the cheek, loving him so much... *even if he has not grown up*, she thought.

"OK. I'm sorry for the nap. Alex worked the heck out of me. I promise I will take no more naps in the shower, and you can take a shower with me anytime," he said with the promise of a connection and desire. Something that he was glad was not lost.

She helped him dry off and changed her shirt, then, drying her hair a little, said, "Food time!" Angel barked, and they both laughed.

"Paul, you have to tell them. Did you see her outside? Did you see how the camera seemed to have a negative image or something? She zoned out for just a second, and it was there. It could have killed him. Did that record?" Alex blurted out. She had been thinking of how to make him tell them all morning.

"You know what happened to my sister. She knew and had told me. That did her no good. I fear that knowing gives it more power. Give me another couple of days. Working with her at night during the sessions seems to help."

"OK. It is your call, boss," she said. Knowing that the boss remark will upset him. They were friends, lovers, and so much more, but when he pulled the my-decision crap, he became boss. She would defer to his judgment on this but wanted him to know what she feared: *We are all going to die.*

## CHAPTER 5
## THE STAIRS

Sarah was still not sleeping well during the day and complained to Jeff as he got ready for his morning session. She wanted to help him pull on his sweatpants, but she let him do it himself since he hadn't asked for help. *If he let me pull them up, I would make him late for his session.* She giggled to herself and made sure not to show it on her face because he would misunderstand. They had not been together since the accident and had been at the mansion for several months. She was not really in the mood this morning but wished he would be soon.

"As soon as I get to sleep, something makes a noise," she said, frustration seeping into her voice. "I just wish I could get a good night's sleep." She took a few sleeping pills, closed the blinds, and said, "Have a great workout this morning." She leaned down and kissed him.

He liked that she called it a workout. Like she used to when he would go to the gym versus calling it rehab.

Quickly turning, she dropped the mom robe and gave him a free show. Then, she jumped into bed and under the covers. She looked up at him and saw his expression; she believed her show had the desired effect. She blushed at her exhibitionism but was happy with the look of desire in his eyes. He felt a good stirring below and said what he hoped was a confident voice, "Today is the day!"

"Let's go, Angel. You get a good sleep; maybe we can shower when I'm back," He turned and rolled through the door and down the hall.

"You ready?" he asked Angel. She looked up at him and barked once in agreement as he approached the stairs.

Angel was in front of him; he leaned down to be face-to-face with her. "You know, the last time I crashed and burned. It did not help when you kept licking my face while I was lying on the ground, OK." Angel lowered her head and made a little woof sound in shame for her actions. Jeff smiled, patting her head, "All is forgiven. Today is the day!"

Angel barked once in agreement.

Using the chair's arms, he stood up, pushed the chair forward, and attached it to the lift. Taking a deep breath, he grabbed the rails and pressed the button to send it down. At the top, he focused for a moment, *thirteen steps, that is all*. Then he looked at Angel, who was always by his side now, "You want to go first?"

She barked twice.

Jeff, hands on the rail, took his first step. Sweat broke out on his forehead. As much in anticipation of the fall as the pain in his hip. "It is in your mind," Alex kept saying to him during their last session. He knew that everything that needed to be removed had been. Most of the pins and screws were gone. They told him everything checked out, and he should be able to walk. The doctors were very impressed with his progress.

"I will not be stopped!" he announced, taking the next step. No doubt in his mind. He held the rail tight and took another step, then another. He knew that Angel was watching him; she waited to lick his face if he fell. He took another step and started to trip but caught himself.

"Focus," he said more to himself. He looked down and saw

he had already made it past where he had fallen multiple times before. The fall started at the second step the first time he tried and ended with him lying about halfway down. Angel rushed down the steps; he was sure at first to check on him, and he was happy that she proceeded to lick his face, covering the tears that he did not want Alex to see.

*One more, just one more,* he thought. He was so upset when he fell, and at the bottom was Alex. He hated her so much then. She had told him, "Stop goofing off and walk down the stairs like a man," and there she had been, just looking at him lying on the stairs. "Fuck you," he called down.

Now, he was further. He needed to be stronger for Sarah. He knew something was strange about this house, about her, and he just needed to be stronger to help her deal with it. He hoped that he would have time.

*One more; it's a step. You can do it. They charged the beaches. You can take one more step,* and he took another. *Stop and rest, yes, that's it. I need a break, but does a fireman stop and rest on the way into a burning building? What type of person am I? I need to be stronger, stronger; fire* burning in his legs, yet he took another step.

The worst part of the fall was not that he fell. It was how he felt and how ashamed he had been of his failure. *How can I protect her if I can't walk down the fucking steps?* He sensed that something was after them, and here he was, laid out on the steps, a failure of a man. Yes, he knew there was nothing to be ashamed of, but when he saw Alex at the bottom of the stairs and the hurt on her face because he cursed her as if it was her fault, he fell.

He turned away from her and crawled up the stairs, His legs useless behind him. At the top, he pushed the button that called for the chair and pulled himself into it, then turned away from the basement.

*No hands, and one more. I can do this. I must do this,* he thought, raising his left and then right hand from the rails. Jeff stood there for a second. He needed to find his balance; for most of the journey down the stairs, Jeff had been looking down; now he looked up and saw Alex, she watched him from the bottom. She was as focused on him as he was. She did not smile; her face was that of stone as she focused all her energy on him.

The first time, in his chair at the top, he turned before rolling away and said one word in German, "Komm!" Angel was confused that he was not coming downstairs but obeyed and came up. Jeff never once looked back at Alex. He did not want her to see him crying, even if they were tears of frustration.

There she was; she looked up at him. "One more step," he said, and she nodded. He put his hands by his sides and took the step, determined not to reach down and them if he started to fall. *Look, Mom, no training wheels,* he thought as he took the next step almost too fast but slowed himself.

Her eyes were locked on his as he took a couple more with his hands at his sides; he was sweating so much now. He could feel the burning in his back and legs as she watched him.

The next day after, he fell, and every day since, he had taken the lift down. She never spoke about him skipping that workout. She would push him from station to station. It was almost as if they agreed to forget that day, and now, here he was, with three steps to go.

"Just three steps, coach."

She smiled briefly and nodded. Inside, she was so proud of him. He had worked so hard and made amazing progress. He seemed driven to her, and it helped; she knew him having a reason to get better helped him focus.

Jeff looked down at her, winked, and put his hands in his pockets. She frowned up at him and held her arms out for a second as if to be ready to catch him. Jeff gave a small shake of his head, and she put them down. "Please, I need this."

"OK," was all she said. She took a couple of steps back to give him room.

"Click, click, boom," he said, then taking the last three steps in stride. Jeff never once looked down; he stopped thinking about the burning in his legs and the pain in his ankles. He was simply walking down the stairs.

At the bottom, she smiled at him, walked over, and, for the first time, gave him a big hug. "I am proud of you, but no more hands in your pockets. You need to fall well if you fall," Smiling, she punched him on the arm and then pulled his chair to him. "Have a seat; you achieved a major milestone. We will work on the next one later, but for now, rest for a minute," she turned her face away and brushed some tears out of her own eyes.

"Angel, come," he said, and she bounded down the steps right up to him; he hugged her tightly and buried his face on her neck, then kissed her head. Then leaned down and let her lick his face clean.

*Excellent way to hide tears,* both Alex and Jeff thought.

Alex turned, pointed toward Angel's couch, gave Jeff one last lick, and went to it. She always listened to Alex unless Jeff objected. Paul purchased a small couch for Angel to relax on during the day. "That hard floor is not good for her, even with the rubber mat," Paul said simply after it was delivered.

Jeff had met him briefly that day. It was very early on, and when he walked down the stairs, he was wearing the same suit he'd had on in the hospital. Jeff had heard of people who always wore the same clothes. This served to take the little decisions in life away so they could focus on bigger issues. *I wonder what his issues are.* Jeff wondered when he looked up at him and said to Alex, "You know, with him only working at night and never out in the daytime, I kind of thought he was a vampire."

Alex responded, "He's much worse," and while it was a joke, it gave Jeff cold chills.

While Jeff was celebrating with Angel upstairs, Sarah had fallen into a very deep sleep. Paul could tell from the cameras that she was about to enter REM sleep, so he pressed a couple of buttons on the keyboard, and inside the floor below her, a hammer hit the ceiling. She stirred a little but did not wake.

"Where did she go yesterday?" Paul asked the empty room.

He looked at the logs and saw that she had gone into town, and then it hit him she had stopped at a pharmacy. "Fuck, no one changed her sleeping pills, and I bet she refilled them!" his voice filled with panic. He hit the button again and again. He knew the hammer was hitting the ceiling, and while it had worked before, now she only stirred a little and did not wake up.

"Fuck. Fuck. Fuck," Paul pressed another button on the keyboard. The lights in her blind darkened room started to flash on and off, going as bright as they go, all the way up to 5000 lumens each. Much brighter than the 800 lumens of a standard 60-watt bulb. He kept an eye on her to make sure that they would be off when she became fully awake; this usually worked, but now, nothing.

He tried both the hammer and the lights together; still there was no sign that she would wake up anytime soon.

"Your legs are cooked for the day. We can do chest and arms," Alex was rolling him over to the bench. He had come a long way from where he had been. He was almost back to his original bench press of 275 pounds.

There were a lot of people who lifted way more, but for Jeff, it was a personal record, and when he reached it again, it felt like things were going his way again. Alex put the weight on the bar while Jeff transitioned from the chair to the bench. He did not use his arms when he transferred to the bench. He would use them to get out of the chair, which most people do in some way or the other when standing from a chair, but he stood, took a step, and sat down on the bench.

Alex was so proud of him and could not wait to tell Paul. *If he is not currently watching,* she thought.

Jeff got under the bar, did his first warm-up set, and then moved on to the second 135 pounds for the last warm-up. He did the first three with no problems. Then he heard Angel bark, and he lost his concentration. The weight started to fall; it came down so fast that he could not resist it. It was then that he saw Sarah; she was holding it down, and the smile on her face told him all he needed to know. She was trying to roll it up from his chest towards his neck. He saw the sharp, jagged teeth as she ran her tongue across them, saliva dripping down.

Alex watched the weight and at first thought that Jeff just lost focus because of Angel's bark. Then she saw Sarah. "My God ... it looks just like her!"

The apparition looked around at her, almost as if it noticed her for the first time and then recognition. Jeff struggled against the weight, his feet kicked up as the bar moved closer to his neck. He could not simply move it side to side to have the weights slide off; they always used locking collars that served to keep the weights on the bar. Early on, he had a couple of incidents where one of his arms would fail, and all the weights would slide off one side, which caused the bar to twist crazily from side to side until it was empty.

As a spotter, it was hard for Alex to prevent a catastrophic failure. Spotters are meant to help with a few pounds here or there. Not an epic failure. They thought about getting a Smith machine, but Alex did not trust them.

Angel was there now. Jeff's feet flailed around, and she could not help. She barked loudly and was then flung back by an unseen force. She flew through the air, and when she landed on her side, Jeff cried out, "No!"

Angel was not done; she rolled over, turned to face the apparition and giving one loud bark that echoed in the basement, she charged.

Alex saw all of this, but she could not move. The Sarah-like being put its other hand on her chest, and her fingers dug through her shirt. She was unable to move. Alex knew that the creature would crush her heart soon.

Paul moved his fingers faster on the keyboard. Paul pressed another command, and the bed collapsed to the floor and then popped up. He added this last. When explaining it to Alex, he smiled, "It's the same technology that allows the muscle cars to raise and lower on the street." He did this again and again, his eyes locked on the monitors. There was no time for him to run down and kill her, or he would. He would sacrifice Sarah for Alex any day, but no time. "Fuck, fuck fuck!"

Angel launched herself from six feet away. Jeff sensed her approach and lowered his legs. Her teeth sank into the Sarah-apparition's arm that it held out to protect itself as it had before, which momentarily freed Alex.

*It knows about the iron, so it is holding her back,* Alex thought and then reached into her pocket, grabbed the small round iron bar that she and Paul both carried. She wrapped her fingers around it, like a roll of quarters used in a fight, and punched the back of its head.

Sarah woke instantly. The bed on the floor was rising up, the lights were blinking, and Paul had no time to stop any of it.

Alex helped Jeff lift the weights off, his hand rubbing his chest. He sat up with a puzzled expression on his face. *She knew. How did she know? She was prepared for Sarah!*

In his command voice, he said something to Angel in German and pointed at Alex. Alex took an unconscious step back in surprise. She did not know German, but recognized the language from when Jeff used it before. She had heard him practicing before, but never that forcefully or directed towards anyone.

Angel moved over and stared at Alex. Angel held her body low and tense as she watched Alex, and it was the not growling, as much as anything that froze Alex in place. She was suddenly terrified by this dog. A dog she had grown to love, and now the dog's master looked at her with such hate.

"What are you doing?"

"You were not surprised by that thing, and more than that, you were prepared for it. Tell me what is going on now, or I swear Angel will tear you to pieces," Jeff said as he stood and moved forward so that Angel's head rested under his hand. *Click, click, boom;* Jeff thought as they faced Alex together.

"We are trying to help," Alex started, and then they both

heard the scream from the stairs. Sarah ran down and yelled, "Jeff? Jeff, are you OK? I dreamed I was killing you!"

Jeff faced Alex, smiled, and said, "I would not move if I were you..."

He turned and walked to Sarah; he had somehow forgotten about his wheelchair for the moment. Sarah ran into his arms and held him, kissed him, and told him about the bed and the lights. They heard the elevator.

Jeff smirked, "I bet we get answers now. Angel, Komm!"

The door opened, and Paul stepped out. Saw them all looking at him; he smiled because Alex was alive, and only stopped when he saw Jeff pointing at him.

"Tell me why I should not have Angel kill you?"

"Because you are standing, my friend, if for no other reason than because of that. It is time we talk, but please, let's go upstairs. It will not be back for a while."

"How do you know?"

Jeff was shocked when Sarah responded first, "Because I am awake."

## CHAPTER 6
## BROTHER PAUL

In the elevator, Jeff sat with everyone around him, including Angel. When the elevator started to go up. No one said a word as they rode. Jeff's legs were shaking a little, but they felt good. He wanted the chair more as a just-in-case rather than feeling like he actually needed it. It had been a long road to recovery, and he knew that he was closer now. Being pissed off had helped.

When Jeff released Angel from her command, it allowed her to relax. She immediately went to everyone to let them know that there were no hard feelings. She was simply a working dog and had a job. One at a time, they all wiped their hands on their pants to get the slobber off, but no one said a word, and no one complained. Oddly comforted by something as normal as dog slobber.

It was when she came back around to Paul to start off a second round of greetings in the elevator that he laughed. When he did, Jeff started to laugh as well. It was that or cry, yell or scream, but he decided to laugh at how ridiculous this must look. All of them so amped up from whatever it was that just happened, and Angel just licked their hands as if she wanted to say, "It's OK, human, nothing to worry about now. It's gone."

The laughter was contagious, and by the third floor, they were all laughing. For Paul, it had been a long time since he laughed like this, and as the elevator opened, Paul bent down to let Angel lick his face; maybe I do like dogs, after all.

Paul leads them to a conference room. Sarah had never seen this room before. There were several monitors around a large table in the center of the room. At the far end of the table was a projector.

Paul sat by the laptop on the table and typed a few keys. Alex turned on the projector, the lights dimmed automatically.

"First, let me say I am sorry that I did not tell you this before. While I am not the cause of your grief; I have known about it for a while, and tried my best to help," Paul said; he looked at them each in turn, even Angel. Jeff had moved a chair away from the table for her. Currently, she sat with her head resting on the mahogany conference table.

Jeff's jaw tightened when he saw the logo on the back of the computer. "Wait a second. Do you work for?" He stopped talking and started to get up. Paul held up his hands in surrender.

"Yes, it was my company that dissolved yours, but please let me talk and all will be explained."

Sarah squeezed Jeff's hand and said, "Please, honey, we will hear him out and if we don't like what he says, Angel will have an early supper."

Paul wasn't sure how much of that was said jokingly, especially when

Angel barked once, but no matter what, he had to tell them; they deserved to know.

"I will start in reverse ... to ease your concerns," he said; the first image displayed on the projector was of a man hanging in his closet. "Apparent suicide is what the police ruled this as. Do you recognize him, Sarah?"

Sarah had turned her head away from the image, not that it was overly graphic. She recognized the scene and had dreamed this. She dreamed about crushing his hands and arms while holding his naked body up until he stopped breathing.

"That's Mr. Sampson; he was our neighbor," Jeff said.

"Sarah, what did he do to you?" Paul asked flatly.

Jeff looked at him strangely, wondering why that type of question.

"Nothing, well, not nothing. OK. Right after we got Angel, he threatened to hurt her if she got in his yard and left a mess. Said, 'I will bury her next to old lady Henderson's cat,' and it made me furious, but Jeff and I were planning to get an underground fence anyway." Sarah shook a little and whispered in a rush, "I thought it was a dream. I remember it all. They said it was a suicide, so I just thought it was a coincidence."

Paul went on to explain that the first coroner was in a rush and did not take the time he should have. Everyone told him it was a suicide, so he just went with it to make it easier. But when a pattern started to form, someone else had a new coroner reexamine the body. "Do not worry. The coroner they called in for a second opinion was private. I will tell you more about him and them later, but Mr. Sampson was killed a month before we talked about the portrait you were doing for me," Paul told them as he projected the next image on the screen.

A young woman with bright red hair smiled in the picture; she had beautiful green eyes, and was wearing a sports top with yoga pants; she was making the universal muscle sign, she posed with both arms out and biceps curled.

Sarah turned her head and pushed her face onto Jeff's chest. Knowing what was next was going to be horrible; after she had dreamed of this girl, she threw up. Head still buried in Jeff's shirt, she turned to the room. Jeff put his arm around her, "I did not know her name."

"Emily," Jeff said as she tensed.

"I picked Jeff up at his gym one day. His car had been acting up, and he had been talking to her at the door. I did not hear the conversation and was not introduced. I stayed in the car, but when Jeff turned that little ..." She stopped herself. "Sorry, I am sure she meant no harm, but she looked him up and down and licked her lips and told the girl beside her she was going to get his number."

"Honey, I never would," Jeff started to say, and she patted his hand.

"I know. It was just when I saw her. I got jealous. Here she was, wearing expensive workout wear, and her hair and nails were done. It seemed obvious she was there to be seen rather than work out. Then you get in the car, and there I am with my hair pulled back, and bits of paint are on my chin and neck from work. You were so sweet and told me I looked so cute, but..." She raised her head back off his shoulder.

"This was six months before Mr. Sampson. Whatever this creature is, it has been with you for a while and has been getting stronger. I am sorry.

I tried to kill it before and thought it died with my sister."

"Please don't, not the next slide, don't," Sarah begged as Paul clicked the mouse and the next image appeared. Emily lay on the bed; she had been burned beyond all recognition, and bits of flesh dripped off her face and breasts, her hair matted to what was left of her skull and her eyes. They haunted Sarah's dreams the most, the missing eyes.

The sheets on the bed were burned as well, but only about an inch away from her body; after that, they appeared to be fine.

"According to the police, she was lying on top of the covers smoking a cigarette and must have dropped it, and it caught on fire," Paul was explaining when interrupted by Sarah.

"But she was naked; what caught fire? And I bet she did not even smoke. Can I get some water? Please, I may be sick," Sarah said in a rush as she remembered the smell of burnt flesh.

Alex stood up and moved toward the door, said, "I will get us all some water and maybe something stronger."

"This is the one that the other group was interested in, and when they contacted me. They had identified you as a possible subject someone needed to watch," Paul clicked the mouse to switch to the next the next slide.

"They are a group of people hunting some type of supernatural entity. They did not tell me much about it, but the deaths are similar to hers,"

Sarah cried "It was my fault."

"No, not your fault, It seems that spontaneous human combustion, which refers to the death from a fire originating without an apparent external source of ignition, is something they watch different news sources for." He paused for a second, he remembered hearing about this from the Man in White and not believing it.

"When authorities labeled the death as 'spontaneous human combustion,' their organization went into action, trying to find out if it was related to their entity. I do not know much about them. When Alex returns with the drinks, We will tell you about my sister."

He paused and nodded to the screen and the photo of a dark-haired, lovely young girl in the arms of her boyfriend or husband. With their ages, you could not tell, but you could see so much love in their eyes as they looked at each other.

"What is happening to you now, Sarah happened to my sister? The reason I did not tell you is that she knew about the entity, and things did not end well. My hope was to try and find something to help you without telling you so that we could stop it. I think that once it knows it is being hunted, it may become more dangerous." Paul stopped as Jeff coughed.

"More dangerous? Seriously? It looks pretty bad so far," Jeff looked at him in disbelief.

"The Man in White, he told me his name, but I cannot remember it. He showed up after my sister's death." Paul paused for a second. They worried about how much this was taking out of him; they could tell how deeply personal this was. "The Man in White wanted to know how she died. He knew some of the history and wanted more details. I hoped that he would help me find and kill it if it was not already dead. I asked him if it returned would they help, but his response was, 'We have our own demons to hunt, but if we come in contact with anything similar, we'll reach out.' I was not pleased at the time, but they were true to their word."

Sarah felt everyone's eyes on her as he stated, "They identified you from some other people in your area." Jeff wondered how many had died or had been hurt but did not ask.

"From my work with my sister, I theorized it was related to REM sleep and tried to interrupt that as much as I could. I know that the being is more powerful when you are sleeping deeply. That is why, until yesterday anyway, I made sure the sleeping pills you were taking were known to keep someone from dreaming. But then you went into town and stopped at the pharmacy. No one thought to mention it to me since it was a quick stop to pick up something else you needed. They never thought of the prescription,"

Sarah looked at him with a knowing look. "You have been changing them every time, haven't you, and the sounds I hear, and the bed today? Jumping like a bucking bronco. You did all of that to keep me from sleeping well. But why the painting?"

Paul smiled. "That was easy. Before you lived here, I wanted something you could work on. I figured if we could interrupt your normal sleep cycle, it would help, and it did for a while. People who work shift-work sometimes complain about not sleeping as well. I also tried everything I could to get you to be upset with me. I wanted you to have it focused on me so that I could study it, and we had some success. The iron bars we carry help, and I believe the iron or salt in Angel's collar helped when you were headed into the lake."

Having thought that it had been a dream, Sarah's voice shook. "That was real?"

"I should have told you. I should have told you that you were driving the car, but I could not believe it," Jeff started to explain and was interrupted as Alex came back into the room with water, beer, and a bottle of vodka.

She had a water bowl for Angel and sat it down on the floor beside her. Alex started to pass out the different beverages according to everyone's preference, and Paul continued.

"It is not Sarah. Jeff, you have to know that deep down. Sarah, we also know it is not you. My latest hypothesis is that it is some type of spirit, maybe a poltergeist, that gets attached to people and feeds on their fears and loves. You see, Jeff, it goes after people who make her mad or who she loves. Strong emotions. I am not sure why. Sarah, remember all that work you had done on the first painting I threw in the fire? Well, it came for me that night. I was lying in bed, and it felt like a vice squeezing my heart, just squeezing. I could not move, and it was looking at me. I could feel it wanted to make me pay for something ... and I even wondered if it recognized me from when it haunted my sister."

Taking a drink and licking his lips, he said, "I am not sure if seeing me confused it, but it did not try to kill me as fast as I had thought it would. It was instead moving its other hand slowly for my eyes. I really do not know why. I felt like it wanted me to see what it was doing as much as it wanted to do it. It just seemed like I had been there for an eternity ... with it reaching for my eyes. I admit not knowing why it gave me the creeps as much as anything we have seen. Why my eyes?"

Paul lifted his glass and stopped when Sarah spoke. "I was going to blind you since you obviously couldn't tell the painting was perfect."

Swallowing nervously, he looked at her for a moment. "Alex saw what was happening on the monitors and deployed several remote weapons we had set up. I needed to know what would work, so at first, it was just small things. A small iron pellet, salt, lead, silver, and even holy water. We have tried a lot of different things with the hope of being able to tell what works as protection or a weapon against it. It does not show up well on recordings. We do not know why, but it can only be seen by its victim and by good dogs."

Angel looked up at the remark, and Paul produced a treat from the tray; he slid it to Angel, who stared at it but did not reach for it until Jeff said, "Treat." Her mouth moved quickly as if the treat was going to get away; she picked it off the table, turned, and curled up in a corner of the room to eat it.

He went on to tell them how they had agreed on a sequence when he saw what weapon appeared to have an impact and what did not. "Alex was watching me closely. We worked out a system based on the fingers of my hand. Whichever would be free. Salt for index finger, iron pellets for pinky, middle finger for cross, etc. Each digit had an action associated with it. The thought was if I could not move them at all to fire everything and pray."

Taking Alex's hand in his, he smiled. "Iron and salt appeared to work the best. Not sure that the old ways are not the best. When she fired the next rounds of iron, it dissipated." Mouth dry, he took a shot of vodka, and the memories of the event were still fresh in his mind.

"I woke up. I remember," I was upset I did not blind you.

"I thought you would. Now, let me tell you about my sister. I miss her so very much. I am sorry that I did not tell you everything before, but promise I was just trying to help," Paul declared apologetically.

He pressed the mouse button to display the next image, and Sarah let out a small scream that drew Angel to her side instantly. The hair on the back of her neck up, and a low growl came from her mouth.

"My sister," he did not bother trying to hold back the tears as Alex picked up the story.

## CHAPTER 7
## HOMECOMING

Tina lit another cigarette. She had not smoked since she had quit at twenty-five when she met her now husband Denny, but here she was chain-smoking. Lighting one cigarette from the last. The flight had been unbearable. The addiction would kick in, she knew, but since she would be in jail or dead anyway soon, what did it matter?

Denny looked at his wife in the passenger's seat. She was taller than he, with long black hair, usually such a beauty, but now she was a shell of herself. The stress of the last couple of days had taken its toll.

It was supposed to be a simple dig. Nothing special. She had been on several over the last couple of years. When their parents died, they had left them more money than they could spend. Paul went into business with the idea of bettering the world, and she started studying archeology to understand it better. Being wealthy allowed her to take these trips whenever she liked.

Usually, Denny would have gone with her, but his mother had recently passed, and he needed to stay behind to settle the estate. His parents did not have much. He had a good-paying job but would never have been wealthy if not for one chance encounter with Tina.

He remembered when he saw her that first day. While shopping, they reached for the same pack of gum. Their hands briefly touched. He looked up, saw her, then made a little bow and said, "This one is yours, my lady. I, being a reformed smoker, will take the next."

She laughed and admitted to him that she was also a reformed smoker. Maybe it had been his smile or the quirkiness of his little bow. "We could split it," she said, laughing, and he joined in.

They started to talk and have been together ever since. The pack of gum in her jewelry box, unopened.

Paul had instantly liked Denny. They could have been best friends if they had grown up together. He was fascinated by Denny's work ethic and skills and begged him to work for him. "The best part is you can take off whenever Tina needs to travel. Please?"

Denny, having never been given anything in his life, found it hard to accept this immediate genuine like and friendship from his soon to be brother-in-law, but they quickly dropped those titles and each became "My Brother."

Sometimes, when they were together, Tina would be jealous of the two. How close they were, but as soon as she would speak, both would focus all their attention on her. Both wanted nothing but to care for her; she had all their love and devotion.

Tina was the youngest, and Paul, being the dutiful older brother, had always done whatever she needed, especially after their parents passed.

"Did you tell Paul anything?" Tina asked, her hands shaking a little.

"Not much ... just that there was a lot of trouble, and we needed help. He asked about sending lawyers, and I told him I was wondering if we needed them or a priest. Now, please relax." Denny said.

"How the fuck can I relax? I have to stay awake, Denny!" she barked and instantly regretted it. She placed her hand on his, the one that had been on her leg, and continued, "I am sorry, but you know what happens when I sleep. I do not know how long I can stay awake, but let's try for the record."

They were silent for the rest of the drive. Tina, in her own thoughts and Denny was trying to figure out what to try and what to do next. He was in computers and technology, and none of that applied here.

Paul opened the door and walked out as they were pulling up. He opened the passenger's side door and smelled the smoke on his sister saw the hollow look, wrapped his arms around her, "Whatever it takes, we will get through this."

He led them inside. Figuring to get the bags later. Denny had been very specific, no one else was to be around. Paul led them to the living room and helped his sister sit on the couch before he took the seat beside her, holding her hand. Denny sat on the other side, arm on her shoulder, while Paul started with a hundred questions---none of which mattered.

In a barely audible voice, Tina said, "I killed someone; no, not someone, everyone." And she hugged her brother and began to cry.

Paul held his sister and patted her back the same way he had always done in the past. He stopped himself from starting a lullaby that their mother used to sing. He was surprised when Tina tensed and sat up. "No-o, can't sleep. I am going to tell you what happened, Paul, and I know you will believe me, but please do not interrupt until I am done. I do not know if I can get through this more than once."

Paul sat, looked at her, and nodded. Taking a breath, she told him about going on the dig, this time without Denny. The dig had been going well; they even found something new. A carved woman's face. "We were in Belize and had permission to dig someplace new. I think that the donations we gave to the different charities contributed to this, but I was not told that directly.

Everyone was just so glad to see us." Tina reached for a cigarette.

Paul almost urged her not to smoke, but after considering how hollow she looked, he went to a shelf and pulled an ashtray off it, one that had belonged to their parents. Their dad was a stock trader, and the ashtray would be completely full by the end of each day. He handed it to her. It's *no wonder he died young.*

She took the ashtray from him and smiled at the shared memory of their father, "The face was a carved stone, about the size of your convertible." As she told the story so vividly, Paul started to see it in his mind. "Denny was to be there the next morning, so it was perfect, but it turned out so wrong!"

"Come, come, everyone, we found it, and she is beautiful," Carlos had yelled, bursting into Tina's tent, exclaiming, "You did it. Thank you for your donations. You did it!"

"What have I done?" she asked, smiling. All of them were smiling. Over at the site, a small ladder led down into the chamber.

"This way, Tina. Let's go down into the chamber," Carlos bid her and she followed.

Talking faster in his excitement than she could understand, he said, "We aired it out; no danger here." He turned and ducked through the small opening.

As she continued to pour her heart out to her brother, it was as if she was living through it again ... Tina ducked as well, and in the chamber on the opposite wall, lit by the lights that had been set up, was a beautiful stone statue of a woman's face. The detail was terrific for a stone carving of that era.

Tina was drawn to the statue's eyes; she walked closer. Carlos was talking, but she was not really listening. The statute was set into the back wall. Its eyes level with hers. The statue's lips were slightly parted. *Whoever carved you was in love,* she thought; she reached out and touched its cheek. Then, having realized what she'd done, she pulled her hand back.

Carlos laughed, "It is OK. We all wanted to touch her. Hell,

Jerry wanted to kiss her ..." And he laughed as Tina bent down and kissed the upper lip of the status. The statue's lips were about the size of her face. That made a funny visual, and she and Carlos laughed.

Never let it be said that Jerry has more game than I do," Tina stated and they both laughed even harder.

She and Carlos both had both taken pictures to document the find and even took the time to pose beside it. Tina stood beside it and felt uneven ground; something was moving under her feet. She gently brushed the dirt away with her hand and saw a small seam, "Carlos, look here," Instead of a response, he placed a brush in her hand, She was able to find the four corners and, with a sheepish grin, asked, "Can I?" In answer, a small hammer with a pick on the end was handed to her.

"If you can, pry it up gently. It is worth a shot," he advised.

She couldn't believe how easily it came up. Later, she would think it was *too easy*, almost as if something wanted out. As she lay the stone lid to the side for Carlos to shine a flashlight in, she felt a cold chill.

Inside was a small compartment about the size of a shoebox. There were several pieces of jewelry and a small urn with something in the center; she wasn't sure what. "Shriveled up heart of her enemy?" she joked, not realizing how prophetic that would turn out to be.

Outside, someone tripped on the cable powering the lights in the room, and they were thrown into darkness. Tina was sure she saw a small animal running towards her. She fell backward and landed on her ass, knocking down Carlos so that when the lights came back on, they were tangled together.

She explained that she had thought she had seen something, and they both laughed. The rest of the day was a blur of photography, documentation, and updating records. They were not allowed to take anything back to the states but had been promised that once things were adequately preserved, the first exhibit in the U.S. would be for a fundraiser to support one of the many charities for which Tina worked so hard.

Tina was so excited it was hard to get to sleep that night. In addition to the findings, Denny will be there tomorrow. "I have to get up early. Denny's coming!" she told Carlos and the others. Making an excuse not to stay up and drink all night with them.

She started dreaming almost right after her head hit the pillows. She could see the woman carving the statue. She wondered if that was usual in her dream---for a woman of that time period to be a sculptor and could see that she was carving her own likeness. The entire time she was carving, she was talking to herself. *No, casting a spell,* Tina realized.

Outside, she heard fighting, but inside, the woman kept working. She heard the screams of people being slaughtered. She thought she recognized Spanish as one of the languages but wasn't sure.

The woman stopped carving, stood, and walked over to Tina. Looking directly at her, Tina could feel the oils being applied to her face, her lips, arms, and even her breasts. "You will die, old woman," Tina said in a voice that was not her own. "Others have tried to imprison me before, but you are done. There is no more time. Your era is at an end, and your knowledge will be lost," Tina declared in that same voice, spitting in the woman's face.

The woman casually wiped it away and plunged the stone dagger she had on her belt into Tina's heart. Tina woke up but could still hear the screaming from her nightmare. She could almost hear the horses. She opened her tent, and there was Carlos. He had a gun in his hand and turned it to her. She noticed ropes suddenly appearing; they wrapped around his arms and legs, and again, she heard the horses as his arms and legs were stretched wide. His body was torn apart, and free from the body, the remains were pulled into the darkness. He'd been drawn and quartered by unseen horses.

Around her, she could see other bodies on the ground. Her

friend Sandy's tent had a large tree collapsed on it. Tina couldn't see anything moving in the tent.

Jerry ran up to her and asked one question over and over again. "Why, why, why?"

She reached out with a hand that was not her own, yanked his tongue out of his mouth, and devoured it. She could taste the warm blood as it went down her throat, and it tasted amazing. She was so happy to be free, *free at last*.

Tina woke up again and hugged herself. "What a crazy nightmare," she said to the empty tent. Taking her time to get dressed, she initially failed to notice the absence of the typical morning camp sounds.

She opened the tent flap, saw the tree down on top of Sandy's tent, saw the blood all around her, and in front of her tent, on his knees, sat Jerry. He was dead, but stared at her tent, she knew. In her dream, she had held his face so that he would keep looking at the tent, unable to call out to wake its occupant in some small hope of stopping the nightmare.

Tina didn't know what to do. She looked to ensure there was no one left she could help. Then, she cried, and she wiped her footprints from around the different bodies. Being very careful not to step on any of the blood was hard. She saw someone hanging in a tree by his intestines above her and somehow resisted the urge to puke.

Back in her tent, she quickly packed all her belongings. There were other tents that were open and, some were just for storage, another partially empty one would not cause too much fuss. She thought about staying and talking to the local police, but having traveled in so many different countries over the years, she knew it was better to argue your case *after* you were safe in the U.S., or at least at the Embassy.

She looked around one last time and then started walking to the road where Denny would be after a detour to Carlos' tent. She took the time to put on gloves, opened his tent, and grabbed the box that she knew contained the documented contents of the site and the room. She grabbed his laptop, the backups, and finally, his camera, along with all the extra SD cards. *I have to figure this out, and if I can't, maybe Paul can;* her thoughts would always turn toward the mainstay of her support system, her brother.

Tina took a deep breath and stopped her telling of the story when Denny told Paul, "I pulled up in the Jeep, she said, 'We have to go. I'll explain on the way.' So now, here we are, brother Paul," Denny finished, using their unofficial relationship for each other, doing his best to smile.

In the conference room, Paul said, "I was amazed that Denny didn't question her at all about what happened. He just took her words as fact. The same as I did. They remind me a lot of you and Jeff, Sarah. I could not help them, but I promise to do my best to help you."

Alex stood up, walked over to Paul, and hugged him. She knew that it had been difficult for him to hear the story, and this was only the beginning.

Sarah looked up at the image on the screen. What upset her before was not how graphic the image was, but the fact Tina was lying naked in a tub full of water. The water was red from the blood from her slit wrists she'd cut. Sarah realized that she must have felt there was no other way to end this, and she cried for her.

## CHAPTER 8
## THE MAN IN WHITE

"After my sister told me the story, I knew it must be true. She had no reason to lie and was not into practical jokes. We started doing research. Money was no object, and we started compiling as much information as possible," Paul said, closing his eyes as he remembered the Man in White.

"'Paul, I don't want to go to sleep,' Tina told me. She was convinced that if she fell asleep, she would change into the other and kill us all. I did not have any way to know for sure if she was correct, so it was agreed that whenever she was asleep, there would be two of us there the entire time."

Alex, my part-time nurse, who I was not as close with then, came to live with us. Everything we did was set up to ensure that when she was asleep, we would wake her if we detected any activity in the house. Alex prepared a shot with adrenaline and Ritalin, as well as some smelling salts. I had the entire house wired for sound, and the mics were always on. This was to prevent it from showing up and us not being able to tell if the person was incapacitated.

"I sent people to Belize to determine what happened and told them that my sister had already left but that we had not received word from Carlos and his team, and we were worried. No one was of any help, and I started studying the compartment's contents. It turned out that it was a heart, and the jewelry, while not of notable monetary value, although it appeared to be very well made, was obvious that it had not come from the region."

Tina slept upstairs during the day with Alex and Denny, and each of them stayed with her. She needed the comfort of knowing they were there, as much as it was for our safety. If anyone saw something in the house, they would wake her. Otherwise, we tried to let her sleep as long as possible.

Looking up, remembering the day well, Paul said, "I was sitting outside when I saw a car drive up. It was noon, and when the door opened, I saw a man all in white getting out of the car. His head was shaved, and his face clean-shaven as well. He looked around nervously before walking up to the porch.' Paul?'"

"He smiled and introduced himself and the foundation he worked for, Explained that he heard about the accident in Belize and wanted to reach out and see if they could help."

"I tried to get more information from him about his foundation, but seated on the porch together, I could tell that we were both holding back some secrets from the other. I did not like the way his eyes kept shifting around, and sometimes, he just looked behind me. It made me want to look around. I wondered if he had something wrong with his eyes."

"Upstairs, Tina was sound asleep now; they saw her eyes blinking to indicate what was believed to be REM sleep. They let her sleep and waited to hear from me ... or some other sign it was out."

"Our discussion done, with no progress on either side, I stood up to shake the man's hand and thank him. 'Give me your number, and I will call if we think of anything else,' I said in parting. He thanked me and handed me a card, then looked over my shoulder, reached out his hand as if ready to shake someone else's, and said, 'I'm sorry, Miss. I didn't catch your name.'"

Shaking at the memory, Paul continued. "I turned, and there stood Tina, but not my Tina. It smiled, and its teeth were all sharpened to jagged points. She reached for the man's hand, but he had already retracted it faster than I would have thought possible. He jumped to the side, his free hand grabbed his chair and slammed it into her. The chair was painted red but made of cast iron, and the creature backed up, hurt, but not enough to be dissipated."

"It reached out for me next, and I swear I heard the horses Tina had mentioned, and I felt ropes on my arms as the Tina thing smiled. I would have expected any sane man to run from this, but the Man in White took the other chair and smashed it against the ground, pulling off one of the armrests to use as a club, he chopped it through the unseen ropes that held me, and they cut the same as if he had a machete and had they been real."

"At the time, I was not in as good a shape as I am now, so I found myself on one knee, slightly winded; he kicked the chair to me. 'Grab a leg or an arm and help me!' he shouted, and I swear to you he was smiling like this was his element. The battle excited him. I remembered that while the inside had microphones, the porch did not, so we were on our own; I twisted the chair, and the leg was freed."

"He moved like a cat looking at the creature. 'What are you? Or, more to the point, who are you?' Outwardly, it did not appear to take much notice of him, but I could tell that it was curious."

"She struck at him with such speed, but he dodged to the left and dove off the porch, rolled, and came up in a martial arts stance. His suit was dusty from the roll, but otherwise, he was intact and unhurt. He smiled again, 'Come get some.' I could not believe it! I did not know who this man was or even what he was if not human, but he was most assuredly not afraid, and that gave me confidence."

"We heard the horses again, and ropes pulled at his arms and legs as he tried to dissipate them with the iron armrest. He was able to get one arm free, but I could see that he was in a lot of pain."

"Well, he's human, at least, I thought as I moved toward her; I hit her several times. I saw the arm go through, and I hoped it was hurting her, but it was not stopped by this."

"He was well off the ground, and I heard a pop and realized that it must be his shoulder or something; I ran, pushed the remains of the chair at her, and jumped to the ground. My ankle popped, an old injury, but I made it to him and repeated the move he did for me, slicing through the unseen ropes. He landed on the ground with a thud, took a breath, and got to one knee. We both looked at the creature; we wondered what to do or try next. That was when, luckily for us, Alex glanced out the window and saw us standing on the ground---well, me standing and The Man in White kneeling. She grabbed the smelling salts first to try and wake her gently, unsure how connected she was to the creature or what damage waking up instantly would do."

"The man got to his feet, glanced at me, and asked, 'This is kind of fun, but how do you stop it?' This was kind of fun. Who was this guy? I thought as we moved toward the creature. It's still stood on the steps as we moved toward it. I started saying hello in as many languages as I could remember. To see if it would respond to any, and it did not."

"Alex, out of fear for us, plunged the needle into Tina, who was then instantly awake, and the creature disappeared. The man brushed himself off with his good arm. His other was hung down. 'We have a doctor ... well, a nurse inside, come on,' I told him."

"'Do me a favor and turn on all the lights first,' he said. He did not explain why; he just asked, and I obliged. 'That is what you were holding back? Interesting. Is it some type of wayward spirit?' he asked."

"'I really wish I knew,' I told him, and we both laughed, moving inside to the conference room. He pulled out a small flashlight and shone it under the table and chair before sitting down. I had not thought of it before, but when we'd been outside, he had turned his chair on its side before he sat down."

"'Problem?' I asked him, and his response was, 'Habit.'"

"We waited for everyone else to come to the conference room. I introduced him to my sister, and after he had overcome the shock of how she looked like the entity, he relaxed. 'They could be twins,' he said to no one in particular. 'I wish we could help. I really do, but what we are after, while deadly in its own ways, follows a different set of rules,' he said and looked at me funny when I said, 'Hides in the shadow?'"

"'You have no idea, and pray you do not. I will not burden you with other strange things that are in this world; know that if we hear of anything like this again or find anything in our records, we will let you know. We, like you, are a private group that have personal reasons for what we do.' He stayed a little while longer, taking pictures of everything we had collected, and offered us suggestions. They were not things that would help get rid of it, but they helped in their own way. I would have offered him as much money as I could to cajole him into staying, but I could tell that this was not his white whale."

Paul saw the questioning looks on everyone's faces when he mentioned 'white whale,' smiled, and added, "Moby-Dick." Then, he picked up the story. "We added more microphones outside, through the house, and in the basement and started researching again. Later, after Tina's death, he returned with his condolences and promised that they would keep looking. He said he had talked to his benefactor and had already been given permission to let me know if it was found in any other place on this earth. In parting the last time, he told me, 'My boss said he would have asked you to join our quest and combine them, but knew that if you are like him, nothing will delay your vengeance, and he would not insult you by asking.'"

"That was several years ago now. As you can see," Paul paused, held Alex's hand up, "we became a lot closer, and even wondered if it did not die when she did."

Jeff stood up at that and stretched, Angel chuffing at him. "I think that someone needs to go out. Honey, let's go take a walk and let the baby out."

"Do you want the chair?" she asked.

"Never again. Thank you, Alex, for this. We will take it slow. I know we have a lot more to hear, Paul. And thank you for trying to help us, but this is a lot to digest. I am sorry for your sister and brother-in-law as well. I want us to review everything you have as quickly as possible and try to beat this," Jeff said, turning and heading for the door.

Sarah said, "No, Jeff. When we get back, he has to tell us the rest of the story his way. There may be something in there that can help us, but also," she reached her hand out and covered Paul's, "you need to heal, and I want to know more about your sister. I am very sorry for your loss." Not sure it was appropriate or why, really, she bent down and hugged him.

Paul shut his eyes, and for a minute, he felt his sister in the room. He started to say something but shook his head, then told them, "We will get some food ready and resume after Angel's walk." Angel, hearing her name, barked once in the hall as if to tell Sarah to hurry up.

When they had left, Alex looked at Paul. "What was it?"

"Maybe nothing, maybe everything. I think I know how to stop it. But I need to think. The cost may be too high. I wonder if I should give the Man in White, a call."

"You keep calling him that, but what is his name?" Alex asked, genuinely curious.

"I honestly don't know. He told me, but I immediately forgot it. I remember every time I talk to him and even use his name when greeting him," Paul lamented.

"Names have power," they both said at the same time, and Paul finished his thought aloud, "Maybe he was protecting himself somehow. I will call him."

# CHAPTER 9
# THE LAKE

Outside, Jeff released Angel, and she put her nose to the ground and did a few circles of the yard before she ran for the lake. Jeff walked behind her, with Sarah holding onto his arm. Strangely, she was happy for the first time in a while. They did not have a solution yet but knew more about the problem.

"Do you believe him?" Jeff asked.

"I do. I can feel a lot of truth in what he is saying and how his sister was feeling. I wish she would have made a different choice." Sarah was interrupted by Angel barking at several ducks she had stirred up. The ducks fly in a slow circle and land in the middle of the lake. Angel looks back at Jeff like he needs to follow.

"Sometimes she looks at me, and I swear she is trying to talk. I know I told you after the accident that she talked to me, and I cannot shake the feeling that she did. What is worse ... I think what she said was important," Jeff told her. He stumbled a bit, but Sarah lets him right himself.

She was amazed at his progress. Alex said that he would recover and had agreed with the doctors that some of it was mental in the end. *Seeing me run over him must have been so hard on him,* she thought.

When he noticed Sarah frown, he misunderstands and said, "I believe him as well. I think he can help us." He squeezed her hand lovingly.

Angel went to the edge of the dock and barked at the ducks. Looked back again, she saw Jeff, who motioned for her to wait, "Last time I was here, it was pushing me," he whispered.

"I know, I was there. It was strange seeing things through its eyes. Feeling its thoughts. I would have tried to stop it but in the moment, I did not want to. I wanted to push you faster. I think some part of me blamed you for getting run over. I know, I know, that does not make sense; forgive me. I think it just puts a lot of thoughts in your head and uses them against you, powering itself. One moment of weakness, wishing you would walk, and it uses that to take control," she said, her head hanging down watching her feet. She did not want to meet his eyes.

Jeff stopped, turned her to him, and said, "I know it was not you. I understand that this is some ghost, spirit, demon, or something, but for me, it was hard at first being alone with you." Then, after a second, he continued. "Wow, I cannot believe I said that finally. I am sorry if I was distant. Just some part of me feared you," Placing his hands on either side of her face, he kissed her deeply.

Angel was barking again. "What?" Jeff asked as they both walk to the end of the dock. Angel was no longer looking at the ducks; she had been looking in the water.

When they kneeled beside her, Sarah on one side, Jeff on the other, resting their joined hands on her back, they looked down, expecting to see a fish, a snake, or maybe a water bug, but what they saw were their reflections. The three of them, but Angel was not there. Between them, it was Tina, their arms around her instead of Angel.

Neither said anything, and neither moved as the image in the water changed. They saw it as if it was happening now but understood that it was before. They were looking at their bedroom. In the bedroom, Denny and Tina was lying on the bed, holding each other. They saw Alex shut the door on the way out and understood that she was giving them some privacy. They both smiled; while they had not beaten the entity, they were managing it.

There was no sound from the images, but they knew and felt the love both had for each other. Tina held him and loved him. Jeff saw that she appeared to feel better. What they were doing was working, and both of them were happy.

Jeff wanted to say "stop" because he knew what was going to happen. He almost screamed at them to stop, though he knew they could not hear him. They remembered the story, how they had thought they had kept the spirit from appearing for a while by not letting her sleep long in the REM state. *But that is a lie*, Jeff thought. It did not need REM sleep. It just needed time to draw energy from its host. It would bide its time till it was ready to strike.

After Tina and Denny had made love, they held each other, and Tina made a joke. Jeff knew it was about needing a cigarette. When she closed her eyes for a second to imagine the taste of a cigarette. Jeff understood but was afraid for them.

Tina only fell asleep for a second, and the spirit had control. Denny did not notice. Jeff could tell that the spirit was maintaining even breathing for Tina. Then Denny said something, and Tina did not respond.

Denny grabbed her hand to wake her and was flung across the room. He is slammed hard into the door. Sarah could see Tina's hands close tightly and Denny's neck compressed; she was choking him. He tried to yell and could not; he was able to move his arms and hammers on the door, which locked itself.

A dresser slid in front of the door, pushed by unseen hands, as Denny was flung to the other side of the room. Like a rag doll, he was tossed back and forth. No sound came from the images, but Jeff could hear the pops of his bones breaking nevertheless.

They did not see the spirit; it was doing this but not in the room, or at least not visibly at first, and then Sarah gasped. The spirit was Tina. She was asleep, but they were one. They had merged into one being. Her eyes open, and it was the spirit in the bed. Not Tina. Her mouth opened, and they could see Tina's straight white teeth, as well as the overlapping image of the spirit's jagged teeth.

The same goes for her body. It was like they were looking at images overlapping each other: Tina's arms were smooth with no tattoos; the spirit's arms are covered in detailed pictures.

They saw the door bouncing on its hinges and knew that Paul and Alex were trying to get in. A few minutes later, the head of an axe came through the door. Jeff imagined Paul wished he had put in cheaper doors but brushed that thought aside as he saw the spirit move Denny directly above her.

Tina---the spirit lay naked on the bed, arms and legs spread wide, palms up, mouth open. Denny floated above her, on the ceiling. The light from the ceiling in a corner of the room where it had fallen when Denny slammed into it.

Denny's arms and legs spread, still naked; he looked down at his wife and the spirit as one. He said, "I love you." Both Sarah and Jeff knew this was what he said, and they had time to wonder how he was still conscious before they came to the realization the spirit wanted him that way.

Wanted Tina to remember everything about this and to remember his pain. Just after he managed to whisper, "I love you," unseen claws dug into his chest. He screamed in pain as his chest opened, ribs cracked, and were thrown aside. Blood rained down on the bed in a torrent, covering Tina's naked body. They saw her open mouth as she sat up. Her hands pushed back her hair, blood flowed into her mouth, and for a moment, Tina was gone. There were only the jagged teeth, only the entity.

They were just through the door when they saw Denny's heart explode. Crushed by the same invisible force. Tina awakened screaming with the knowledge that Denny was dead. His lifeless body fell on top of her. She felt the warmth of his blood and body all around her.

Sarah started to say something started to move but sensed there was more here that was important, so when Jeff began to move as well, she squeezed his hand to keep watching.

Paul and Alex enter the room and the scene shifts. They knew that time had passed in the vision. Tina looked worse than she had before. A shell of herself, almost hollow. She was smoking again and barely moved.

They helped her move from the bed to the rocking chair to the bed and shower. Always talked to her. Always loved her. Paul read to her whenever she was awake. 'Moby Dick' is the title easily seen in the vision.

Jeff and Sarah could see the budding relationship of Alex and Paul. Going through this with someone, *they will be together forever*, both thought.

Tina was helped everywhere she went. They continued to try to keep her from falling into REM sleep. They still did not understand how it was freed when she was with Denny. Paul was at a loss for an explanation and could only conclude that he must have fallen asleep as well and that they'd been asleep longer than they'd thought. Alex had turned off the videos in the room for privacy, not understanding how quickly things could happen.

Sarah was not sure how she knew this from just watching the vision, but she knew what they were thinking.

*They will understand shortly,* Jeff thought. Things in life happen quickly, and you have to plan for everything and adjust. *That is what we must do! This is why Angel is showing us this!*

The vision shifts. Tina was now in the bath, hot water around her with Alex, sitting beside her on the floor, holding her hand. Jeff noticed first, and then Sarah did too. Tina's eyes slid shut for just a second, and then she said something and made a smoking-a-cigarette motion.

Alex shook her head, and Tina started to cry. Alex stood and did what anyone with compassion would do; she went to the bedroom to find the cigarettes.

Jeff could see the indecision on her face but knew that he may have done the same thing. He knew Alex was still under the assumption of the REM sleep theory as she struggled with this decision.

When Alex was out of the room, the door shut slowly and locked, apparently on its own. Tina's arm spread wide, the medicine cabinet door opened apparently by itself, and scissors floated through the air toward her arm.

Sarah looked into Tina's eyes; Sarah could imagine seeing this in her own dream and almost screamed but did not want to miss anything that may help them all.

The scissors sliced through her arm first, from the wrist all the way to the elbow, and then they went beneath the water, and Jeff imagined them slicing an artery in the leg. The entire time, Tina was smiling with those jagged teeth, and her eyes screamed.

They saw the door move and knew that it would not be long before she was found. Tina slumped in the tub in the throes of death, and they saw something rise from her. It was so beautiful. Both of them imagined it was her soul. As the door burst open, they saw a darker object ooze out of her and disappear through the wall.

Angel barked, and Jeff and Sarah both shook themselves back to the present. They saw their normal reflection was back. A man, his wife, and their good dog, but she is so much more.

Their hands still joined on top of Angel's head; Jeff said, "I thought she said her name was Angel. She must have said she was an Angel," and both laughed when Angel barked once in agreement.

"We have to tell Paul his sister did not kill herself," Sarah exclaimed.

"Yes, and this spirit was more dangerous than we knew. Let me see your teeth," Jeff said and laughed at the last bit. He meant to use humor to ease the tension, but it fell flat. "I'm sorry, honey. I love you, and we will beat this thing. That vision was just, wow, you know."

Angel bark once before turning and leading them back to the house, Alone on the dock they kissed again, and followed Angel.

They met Paul and Alex in the kitchen. Paul was cooking while Alex watched. The speed and skill he displayed in the preparation made both of them believe he must have had some training. Paul sliced off a piece of steak he was cooking and tossed it to Angel, who, after eating it, looked up for more. She sat beside him and carefully watched for any stray pieces of steak that may fall.

# CHAPTER 10
# **REVELATIONS**

After supper, they went back into the conference room. Sarah had only eaten a little. Knowing her body, she did not want to take a chance and nod off; she knew that was not the only way to turn, but she did not want to take a chance.

As everyone was seated around the conference room, Angel took advantage of the opportunity and went around the room to allow all the humans to pet her. Paul was surprised that she ended up beside him on her journey.

*Looking for more steak,* he thought as she laid her head on the conference table as she had done earlier with Jeff.

They all sat quietly with the projector off as Paul mentally prepared to talk about his sister. Absentmindedly, he put his hand on Angel's head and gently scratched again; instantly, he felt that connection with his sister and smiled.

"We need to tell you what happened at the lake earlier," Sarah said, and both Alex and Paul tensed. Not pleased they had waited till after dinner to talk about anything.

Sarah did the talking; she felt it was her duty to talk about it, and she did. She left out nothing; she even explained how when they first got the puppy, they did not have time to give her a name. She told them, "Jeff swore Angel had told him her name. As it turned out, he may have misheard. I don't know if it is possible or not---"

She was interrupted by Paul; tears filled his eyes; he said, "She is my sister or at least a part of her. I have felt it for a while." He leaned his face down against Angel's as he let out tears and a lot of emotions he had kept bottled up. He looked down at her after he composed himself, "I am sorry I failed you."

Angel barked twice, her typical negative response.

Alex took Paul's other hand in hers, "We failed you."

Angel barked twice and looked up at them.

Sarah, who had barely held back tears, said, "No one failed her or me. You did not have all the facts," and she told them of the vision, took a breath, and, looking at them, finished with, "We still may not have them, but we will be more prepared."

"You are right," Paul agreed, then looked at Angel, "I feel her in there, but it must be so hard for her to get it out for us stupid humans to understand."

Angel barked once, and they all laughed.

"While you were out, I made a couple of phone calls. I have an idea, and I want to be prepared. Now that we know that the spirit can be in the room with us while you appear to be awake, I am glad I waited until you were out," he told them.

"Thank you for telling me about the vision and trusting me to help you," Paul said while keeping his hand on Angel's back. The casual way a sibling would when relaxing on the couch watching TV more than that of someone petting a dog. He felt her energy more now. *Whatever is going to happen will be soon.*

"When Alex told you the story of what happened, I believe I may have found something. That's why I made the call ... to have something prepared. Luckily, the Man in White had already been working on something like this for one of his own demons, and he said he was happy to help."

Paul looked down, Looking down at Angel, who yawned, "Now, with what you said, I believe when the spirit killed my sister, it was trying to free itself. I think you saw it. I had always been under the impression that my sister did it to try to protect us."

He started to tell them his idea. "If we can get the spirit out and maybe trap it while it is between bodies, we may stand a chance."

A hopeful smile on his lips, "We may be able to be rid of it, if not kill it." Paul turned on the projector and started to show them all the pictures from the camp, and even brought in the jewelry and the heart.

Supper, having been several hours ago, Sarah barely held in a yawn. Paul nodded his head toward Alex. Alex walked over to Sarah, producing a needle from her bag. "Sarah, this will keep you wide awake. You will feel like you have had twenty cups of coffee. I know that it may not be the REM sleep, but your being awake may help. It should give us the time we need. I must warn everyone after about five hours, she will crash hard. Are we ready for this?"

Paul looked at his watch, "Five, yes," he frowned, remembering that Tina had given it to him. Paul continued to talk, but Sarah was finding it hard to focus on him. She was finding it difficult to focus at all; looking around the room, she hoped that someone would look in her direction, but no one could see her distress. Her eyes were blurred, and she feared that it was the spirit coming up. She felt sweat break out on her forehead and wanted to warn them; she leaned forward, "Hel ..." then passed out, her head almost hitting the table as Alex, knowing what was going to happen, caught her.

"Now!" Paul screamed as the conference room door burst open.

"Quickly," the Man in White said to his people, who came rushing into the room.

Jeff stood and pulled Sarah to him, but the men quickly yanked him back, and they placed Sarah on the table. Jeff shouted something in German, and everyone froze as Angel growled.

Paul looked down at her and said to both her and Jeff, "Please trust me; we have to get it out of her."

At those words, all of the tension left Jeff; he had no choice, "Please help her."

The Man in White's people started to erect a small box around her. "Not a coffin!" Jeff screamed, still being held by the others who entered the room.

Angel could do nothing but guard him.

"It is of a sort, but only for a little bit. Do you have everything else prepared, Alex?" Paul asked, his hand firmly held onto Angel's collar. She was not fighting him but looked at Jeff for a signal. Paul thought it was to wait for his command to attack, which never happened.

*I can feel my sister in there, but Angel is a dog, so who knows how that works?* Paul hoped that Jeff would not keep fighting.

"She has to die, and then we will bring her back. They have put her in an iron enclosure. We figured out that iron worked, so Mr.---fuck, what is your name? Anyway, he built this box and also the van. We are taking a chance here, but from what you said, the spirit will leave her body soon after she dies. When that happens, we will bring her back. How long was it in your vision after death?" Paul asked Jeff.

Jeff, hate in his eyes, growled out, "Two minutes at most."

Paul looked at his watch again and marked the time. Everything went eerily silent, and at two minutes, said, "Now!"

Jeff had not noticed the people bringing in the five gallon bottles of water, and now they poured it into the coffin. The water was not clear, Paul said "Salt water. It will leave a small area at the top. Sarah will be covered in salt water."

Jeff looked on as Paul kept checking his watch, after what felt like hours, Paul yelled, "Now!, Insert the panels and get her out of there!" The Man in White handed Paul a thin metal panel and found the notch in the side; the panel slid into the seam. The action reminded Jeff of a magician cutting someone in half, but this was lengthwise in half. He heard it catch a few times, as Sarah's body must have floated until it made a satisfying click as it locked into place.

He produced two wrenches from his pocket, and together, they finished bolting the panel in place and made sure the seal was airtight. As part of the same process, they disconnected the top portion of the coffin.

"We do not know much about the entity, but from what we know, it does not stay long in a dead or dying host. So, with the mixture of salt and holy water in the coffin that covers her body, when we remove the top completely, she should be free of it."

Once the top was detached, The Man in White's men carried it out, moving carefully. Water covered the table and floor; Paul and the Man in White lift Sarah, from the coffin, placed her on the table; there was no mistaking the absence of life.

Paul looked up and saw the top half being carried into the elevator. The Man in White, a look of determination on his face,

"Now, bring in the rest!"

Jeff was amazed at how fast the medical people came in; soaked as she was, they stripped her and dried her as best they could while different injections were shot into her body. They had her on air, and Alex was doing CPR.

Paul glanced at Angel, she was still seated, her face looking up at Jeff, *If he had told her to attack, would her instincts have taken over?*

Alex frowned and called for the paddles. They set them and yelled, "Clear!" before shocking her body. Alex checked for a heartbeat and then again and again until finally, on the screen, a little blip appeared, and then another and another.

Everyone took a calming breath, and Paul turned to Jeff,

smiled, and then started to frown when Jeff punched him in the face, then followed it up with a kick to the groin.

Paul, lying on the ground held himself, was surprised when Angel stepped in front of him and growled at Jeff.

"I'm sorry. I could not tell her, and you two were never apart," Paul said, taking more time to get off the ground than it should have. *He has a hell of a punch.*

"How is she doing?" Jeff asked Alex.

"Good. We have no way of knowing if this worked until she goes to sleep, but it was the best we could do," she responded.

The room was quickly cleared, and Alex, Jeff, and Paul, along with the Man in White, moved to the room next door. Angel followed them through the control room to one that was set up like a hospital room.

Sarah was moved from the stretcher and placed on a hospital bed.

"I sometimes use this room when working late. I had it configured with this equipment in case we needed it for you." Paul said in the form of an explanation.

Sarah was still not conscious. Jeff stood beside her, head down, and held her hand in his. The Man in White discussed the options for the coffin with Paul. "We have to bury it deep where no one will ever dig it up again."

"Agreed," Paul said, feeling it was more of a formality the question.

"We have some facilities we can use. It may be time you met our founder," the Man in White said, he nodded to the rest of the room, and shook Paul's hand. "I need to check on my team, and make sure everything is secure in the van."

The van had been specially designed. The back of it could be removed. Initially, it was configured up as a small compartment inside the van, similar to a room with lights all around, that they had used for another purpose, but when he found out this spirit was active again, he'd had the van modified and stored close by.

It was only luck that he was here today. He had been checking on a possible shadow sighting when Paul had called.

Outside, he watched his people bolt the iron coffin inside the small iron room in the back of the van. This had been his idea, and he was glad it had worked out. His backup plan if they could not separate the creature from the host was to grab the host and, once in the iron van, decide what to do. There had been enough death.

Jeff turned around, and started to sing "Click Click Boom" by the band Saliva, a song that had been caught in his head since before the accident.

Paul and Alex wondered what he was doing. They saw his other hand on Sarah's throat slowly squeezed.

"Others have tried to stop me. What made you think you would be successful?" the spirit said through Jeff.

Alex reached for the iron bars she carried, but before she could pull them out, Jeff, or what used to be Jeff, picked her up and threw her out of the third-floor window. She crashed through the glass and screamed all the way down until her voice was cut off when she hit the ground.

Paul had reached for her but was thrown against the other wall. Then slammed against the floor and ceiling as the spirit Jeff laughed and said, "Little Man, you thought you could help them. You couldn't help your sister. What did you expect? You are only human."

Paul struggled and tried to get the metal bars out of his own pockets; Paul felt like an old rag doll and could not get the vision of Denny out of his head.

The Man in White and his team ran for the door. He directed the medical team to check on Alex. *I knew this was too easy*, drawing the pipe out of its sheath. All of his team members had been equipped with them for this job. In addition to the flashlights they always carried, this would become a standard feature in their arsenal.

The spirit Jeff cackled, "You humans are all alike. When you tamed fire, you thought that you could tame the world. I loved watching your ancestors burn when they got too close!"

Paul, pinned to the ceiling, felt his shirt ripped open and knew that he was going to die. He smiled and gave a little choked laugh.

"What?" Spirit Jeff demanded, his spiked teeth showed. Paul only laughed; it was then that Spirit Jeff turned and saw where Paul was looking. Angel, who had known something was off with her Master ever since the lake but was unable to communicate it--- leaped for Jeff's throat. The weight of the dog threw the spirit, Jeff, backward, and unable to maintain balance, it fell onto the wooden floor.

Angel, a Mastiff, had a bite strength of 552 pounds. This is just short of a lion as it and as it clamped down on the spirit of Jeff's throat, it squeezed.

Paul fell to the floor. Fear gripped him. He had to stop himself from running to the window and looking out to see if Alex was dead or alive. His love for her and his rage at the entity was all that kept his broken body going.

He was relieved when looking up to see that Sarah's heart was still beating. *That is one for the home team.* Paul gathered all of his remaining strength, used the bed to pull himself to his feet, and stalked toward Spirit Jeff.

Angel had Jeff pinned to the floor, so Paul bent down and started to smack his face repeatedly; he hoped that this would wake him and bring him back.

The Man in White and a few of his people entered the room and spread out, took in the situation, Angel's, her paws on Jeff's chest, head turned, muscles tense, her mouth still locked on Jeff's throat, and Paul going down to one knee, as he continued to smack Jeff in the face. "Is the van outside still?"

"Yes. Want us to carry him down?" The Man in White asked.

"No, go back down; you will know what to do," Paul replied.

Outside, the medical team had Alex stabilized. Luckily, she hit a tree that slowed her fall to the ground. Her body was scratched and bruised, but unless the scans showed anything, she was lucky. They were finishing up with her, and they looked toward the window, wondered what the team inside had found.

She was surprised when the Man in White and his team came out of the door. The look on his face, grim. He back, and up toward the window she was thrown out. Her eyes naturally followed; "Noooooo!" she screamed.

## CHAPTER 11
## ANGELS AND DEMONS

Paul stood up, took a deep breath, and tried to clear his mind for what he must do. Through tears of pain, he saw Angel with her jaws still locked on Jeff's throat; beside her, his sister wore white robes and golden armor with silver trim. She was so beautiful. One of her powerful legs stood on the demon's throat; Paul now saw it clearly.

Tina's hand was pointing at the demon on the floor. He knew it was a demon now. Not sure how, but he knew this. Her other hand raised toward the heavens, a flaming sword in it. The look of determination on her face reminded him of when they competed against each other as kids. She always had this same look of determination on her face. He had not let her win often when they played, but he did some and never told her. He always complained when he lost, but the joy on her face back then was so incredible to see. He missed her so much; her success in life was all that meant anything. At least before Alex.

She had taken this determination to her hobbies and into her life, and Paul had been so proud of his sister. Tina had not been looking at him but did then. Their eyes locked, and he saw the walls around them dissolve. There were only the two of them;

they stood in the darkness together, the only light from her sword; it barely pierced the blackness.

There was a burst of light, a star exploding, and he saw the shadows more clearly. Some burned instantly, some ran, a few hid, and some tried to stop the light. But the light would not be stopped.

Paul looked up towards the light and saw giant birds; they flew down, and he smiled when he realized *They were angels.* Their wings were broad, white, and gold with a hint of purple, and for the first time, he noticed his sister's wings. They were close against her skin but so lovely.

The angels drove back the shadows and demons, forcing them deep into the earth or other realms. Some fought back; giants threw huge stones at the angels. Titans, their muscles rippled as they struck with swords that appeared to be made of the darkness itself.

Paul knows the name of every entity and felt it must be his sister imparting this knowledge to him.

The titans surged forward, led by the Nephilim, and he saw several angels fall. He wept for them. A colossal demon, Asmodeus, a prince among the demons, laughed as it swung a giant flaming sword; it cut down several angels. Paul winced with their pain.

Other demons, shadows, and creatures from different nightmares rose up, encouraged by Asmodeus to take the fight to the light. He understood their plan to strike the light and bring back the darkness.

In a rush, all of the remaining forces of the dark charged the angels. No, not all. Paul focused and saw one that cowered at Asmodeus's feet; as Asmodeus moved closer to the light, it found a Titan's piece of armor to hide under.

Paul felt its fear and knew with the same certainty that he knew everything in this otherworldly experience that this was the demon that killed his sister. Paul wished he could pick up a sword and strike the creature dead.

The angels fought well, but Paul knew the lines would break soon, and then he saw them. The angels felt pride and relief when the humans joined the fight. At first, they carried rocks and clubs, and then, as more joined the battle, they had short bows.

The longbows and swords changed over time and, eventually, more advanced weapons, guns, and canons. Paul wondered *If this battle was still happening. Even now?* Then he saw movement where his demon cowered.

A woman fell beneath a Titan's spear. She had been a powerful sorceress. Paul knew this, and she had been fighting for the light; she lay there, gasped for air, and the demon smiled. The demon looked around and saw the tide of the battle had turned. The great giants that had not run were all dead. The titans had all fallen, and the Nephilim were retreating. Other creatures of the darkness fought on but were easily killed by the angels.

He noticed that more and more of the angels were flying back into the light, and thought this must be the age of humankind on the earth. "The battle and choice is ours." humanity said as one.

The demon crawled out from under its hiding place and approached the sorceress whispered to her and promised her everything, and she shook her head no.

The demon went back to hiding and watched, studying the sorceress. In studying, her thoughts were open to him, and the final thoughts she had were of her son, who had been killed by another demon. The demon smiled and took the shape of her son.

He slid toward her, scared to let the light see him. He reached out his hand and, grasping hers, "Mom, you are at rest; kiss your son and be at peace." She did, and the demon entered her. Her wounds instantly healed, and she stood. No other humans had noticed this as the spirit sorceress joined the battle on the side of humankind.

Paul's vision cleared, and he was in the room again. He

looked up at his sister, "I know what I have to do. I wish I could have been there for you in the end."

"You were always there for me when it counted. It would be best if you acted soon, dear brother. It is ancient and stronger than it has ever been," Tina warned.

He smiled at her, "I love you," then crawled like the demon had toward it on the ground. Paul his face inches from the demon's. "Come into me. This vessel is yours," Paul said, kissing the Jeff-Demon on the lips.

Nothing happened at first, and then he could feel the demon enter him. It may have been because he had willingly offered himself or that it understood Paul's promise and challenge.

Paul stood up, looked down at Angel, and briefly scratched her on top of the head as she let go of Jeff. His sister's spirit was still with him, he knew, but he could no longer see her. Maybe it was the demon inside of him that prevented this; he repeated his words from before, "I love you," then, while he still had control, took two steps and dove out of the already broken window.

Alex saw him jump and screamed, "Paul!"

She tried to get up to go help him but was restrained by the medical staff. The Man in White ran over to Paul with another member of his team, and together, they grabbed him, lifted him, and, paying no attention to his injuries, carried him toward the van. "We can try the coffin?" The Man in White asked.

"No," Paul moaned. "It knows that trick, and it would simply stay with me until I was dead. We have to move to Plan B. Or was it C?" he laughed, which turned into a cough mixed with blood from his injuries.

"I am holding it in right now. I had some tattoos put on early when my sister was here, and I think they are helping to protect me from them. Who knows, though? It could just be tired from fighting my sister." When Paul said this, the Man in White looked at him, confused.

In the van they put him in, they pointed out the medical

supplies in the back. They could not take the time to treat him but hoped to give him some comfort.

"There is also a revolver," the Man in White said almost apologetically, but he knew that if it were him, he would want the option. "Only one shot, just in case it gets away. I don't think the round will do any damage to the iron lining of the van, but we can't take a chance. We can talk more when we get you back to base. There is also food and water." All of this was said in a rush as they were getting out of the van themselves.

Alex escaped the two medical personnel who'd been holding her down and moved toward the van with incredible speed, considering her injuries, "Paul!" she cried.

As the doors shut, he yelled back, "I love you! Only choice. Sorry, my love!"

She screamed and knocked down two of the men, who tried to get between her and the van, but the Man in White held his arms out wide, and she collapsed into his embrace. She was cursing and crying and screaming, and he held her through all of it.

The other members of his team were already moving upstairs to check on Jeff and Sarah. Alex put her hand on the van knowing that inside, Paul would be doing the same. "Stay alive for me," she yelled as the van pulled away.

"Where is it going?"

"To one of our facilities. I will take you there later," he promised, still holding her, he motioned for a medic to come.

Alex spoke through the tears and frustration. "They may not be in the helping mood," The Man in White held back a smile. One of the medics was holding a towel over his nose, and another was holding his wrist.

With a nasal voice, the medic said accusingly, "You broke it."

"Good," Alex said, not stopping at the porch; she wanted to go inside.

Upstairs, Jeff was seated on the floor; he rubbed his neck. Angel whined; she wanted to get him to hold her. He kept telling her it was OK and Angel only stopped when he held out his arms; he kissed her on top of her head and felt the nervous slobber on his pants. Angel, happy now, laid her head on his lap, panting.

"Good dog," he croaked his voice would not be the same for a while.

Jeff looked up while absentmindedly petting her with one hand; he nodded his head at Alex and the Man in White when they entered. Alex moved to Sarah first and found her vitals were strong. "She will be awake soon," she said, then got on her knees beside Jeff to check on him. He noticed her injuries as well and her wince but did not mention it.

"You are lucky. She could have crushed your windpipe," Alex said when Jeff told her what happened. Angel had wined and was upset that she had to hurt her master.

Angel did not want him to talk about it, and Jeff understood, "You are a good girl, Angel. You saved us and did exactly what we needed," Jeff said. Angel barked once, then laid her head back down.

Jeff told them what he remembered and recalled feeling something when they kissed the last time and thought it was just his toes curling as they always did when they kissed, but when they walked back to the house, he found that he was unable to say certain things. I tried to say, "We have to tell Paul," he said.

He looked around, and remembered Paul had jumped out of the window. Looking up at the Man in White, "Can you help him? Sarah and I will do whatever we need to help him and you; we owe you our lives, and I don't even know your name," Jeff said.

The Man in White laughed and told them. Jeff, upon hearing the name, chuckled to himself and wondered how Paul could not have remembered a name like that.

The Man in White handed him a card and told him to call if they needed anything. He scratched Angel on top of the head before he turned to leave. As he passed through the doorway,

Jeff went to say goodbye, followed by his name and can't remember the Man in White's name to finish the farewell.

Looking at Angel, "Do you remember it?" Angel, asleep on his leg, did not respond.

"Write it down next time; yes, let's do that," Jeff said, nodding his head in the affirmative.

"Now, I assume you are going to pack and head back with them. Can we stay here for a few more days?" he asked.

"The place is yours. Well, ours. Paul, when he called them, told them to draw up the papers for him, and he signed them. I didn't know he was doing this, but evidently, he figured out that if we could not fool it into coming out, there was a chance that it could switch bodies," She only stopped her retelling when Sarah began to wake.

Paul could feel the van turn onto the interstate. He had never learned where their local facility was, but he was thankful that they had prepared. "Wish I would have known them earlier," he said to the empty van.

He had been holding the pistol in his hands since the doors shut. Part of him wanted to do it and let the creature rot inside this van for eternity, but he wanted to see his sister and Alex; he still believed if he took the coward's way out; he would be no better than the demon now inside him. He unloaded the revolver. Pulled the cylinder out of it and used the side of the coffin to break the hammer off; this would remove any temptation, and also not give the demon a weapon.

Paul wrapped his wounds and put his hands back behind his head; he laid down and said to the demon, "I have been fighting you for a long time. How about we get to know each other."

# AFTERWORD

Paul sat in his rocking chair, reading a book. It is one that he has read before, but he enjoys it. He used to read it to his sister when she was young. He heard a noise from the speaker on the desk and looked up. The signal was alright, given he was in an iron room. At least he did not have to use Morse code by banging on the walls.

"Paul, can you hear me?" Alex's voice came through the speaker. "I am working with Thomas." There was a muffled sound, and she continued. "Sorry, Tommy and his father constructed this and a couple of other facilities to fight something else," she explained.

*The shadows,* Paul thought, but did not say it.

"I believe we will be able to get video soon, and we are still working on ways to cure you."

Paul did not respond. He looked down at his self-bandaged arms. One of them was in a splint made from the legs of a wooden chair that had been in the room. The demon had shattered it the first night in a fit of rage. It had shattered everything it could. Though it did not injure Paul as much, it refused to let him heal. Every time it took over and found something close to being healed, it would rebreak it. The demon always stopped

## AFTERWORD

just short of trying to kill him because it knew that Paul was its only hope of getting out. However, it did vent its frustrations. It had even torn pages out of his book for spite. That was the thing that gave Paul the most hope. The fact that the demon could be petty made him think it was less powerful than they had feared.

He sat up a little straighter in the iron rocking chair; he noticed its similarity to the ones on his porch. "How long has it been?"

"Six months," Alex responded. She had this question from him every day she visited and knew that it was difficult for him to mark time, so she gave him the exact date and time.

"How are they? Sarah and Jeff, and Angel?"

"Good, still surprised that you gave everything to us. They do not really know how to be rich yet. Sarah still does coupons before she shops. They will be OK. Angel is good. I am not sure if your sister's spirit is still with her or not, but she is an amazing dog," Alex said, then updated him on some business decisions he needed to make. He knew he would have to make them in the future, but he was not ready for that. Alex was unsure what to say. She had said everything she needed to tell him but had not stated all she wanted to say to him for so long now, "How could you do this to me? How could you leave me all alone?"

She did not say those things because she knew that they would hurt him, and cause him even more pain. She knew what he did was the only choice for him.

"The setup of the room worked out perfectly," he told Alex. "We figured that the demon could not move or hurt anything covered in iron or salt. They have a panel they can open if mine is shut for food and supplies. The spirit made a mess the first couple of times but has settled down. I think that it is studying me as much as I am studying it. Sorry. I know I have told you this before. I think it is making me forget things,"

Paul stated he did not say the things he really wanted to say, "I love you. I need you." And what he wanted to say most of all but won't, "Wait for me." He knew that it would not be fair to

## AFTERWORD

her, and he did not want to put this burden on anyone else with this life.

Tommy had suggested finding someone dying and offering to pay their family if they would switch places with him, but Paul pointed out how his injuries, while still painful, healed at a remarkable rate... except for his arm, which the demon prevented purposefully.

A death like the one they'd given Sarah would be an option, but again, it knows that old trick now and may use the chance to escape into someone else.

Alex looked at the speaker and wished they had video. At least then, she could see him and know more than what he reported about his body. "Tommy promised me that if we help him with some financial resources, they will treat you as one of their top priorities. I have agreed. I did not want to know what they were fighting before. I hoped to find something to help you on my own but could not. He told me what they were fighting but said, due to the limited light in your room, you are better off not knowing. I know. All mysterious, but it's for the best, trust me."

He trusted Alex and even Tommy. Having only heard his voice. When Alex mentioned the light, he looked around the room at part of his daily supplies, which were battery-powered lights. At first, the demon had destroyed these as well but stopped when it realized this had no impact. Paul piled them in the corner until it was time for trash day.

Other waste was kept the same. They would lock his side and remove the compartment completely, and according to Tommy, "They would bury the waste very deep."

This way, even if the demon tried to escape unknown through the trash, it would not be free.

Air and other things were piped in through similar mechanisms, and Paul had been made as comfortable as he could be, with no request for a specific type of food or book ever refused.

Paul asked in a tiny voice, "Photos. I would like to have some

# AFTERWORD

photos from my albums, as well as some of Sarah, Jeff, and Angel's. It will be good to see their lives." He took a deep breath and said something that was harder for him than he could imagine, "Not one of you, my darling. If I see your face every day, not being able to hold you, I will go crazy. For now, just them and my past, please."

Alex tried not to cry in front of Tommy and the Man in White but could not help herself.

Paul sat the book down on the rocker's arm, shut his eyes just for a second, and felt the demon take over. He let out a gasp, hoping they noticed the change. "Alex, please send a picture," the demon said in a soft, seductive voice. "Send some of those sexy pictures, or come and visit. I am awake now; no chance of the demon. Come and see me. If you love me, you would come and see me and not leave me here to rot," hearing the creature using Paul's voice hurt her more than she would ever let the demon know.

Even if Paul had not made the noise, they would have known. After Jeff had become infected, which was the only word that fit for a scientist, they would listen for any change in attitude or voice. They should have known with Jeff when Angel shied away from him, but too much had been going on at the time.

"Please, honey, I beg you, remember our trip to ..." And it continued on and on, trying the sweet, seductive voice. Then, when it saw that it wasn't working, it went the opposite way. It used all of Paul's knowledge of her and some of the different insecurities that everyone had to hurt her.

Alex did not move. She shed no tears for what it was saying. She did not become embarrassed when things only Paul knew about her were revealed; instead, she focused on finding a way to kill the demon.

"Paul told us how you were whimpering while all the other powerful creatures fought the angels. There you were, in a

## AFTERWORD

puddle of your own filth, whimpering and hoping you would not be noticed. Well, now we have noticed you."

Alex nodded to the others in the room and left with Tommy and the Man in White. Two trusted technicians were left to monitor the speaker and the room as much as possible. "Is it always two?" she asked.

"Yes. We found that if we had a single point of failure with the other creatures, they were likely to find it. With this demon being so creative, we did not want it to be able to entice one of our techs into betraying us," Tommy explained, then pressed the button to call the elevator.

Tommy, before he got off his floor, hugged her and thanked her for coming and being a part of the team. "He will help get you up to speed. When ready, bring Sarah and Jeff out; we can brief them. They should know about the threat, even if they do not want to help more than financially. Just do not tell them anywhere but in the light," he advised, broke the embrace of their hug, and left.

Tommy walked to his office. On the shelf was the boombox that he used to kill the first shadow creature. Winding it up, he let the song play. It had been a lot of years since he started this, and he needed to find a new generation to continue the fight. He had hoped it would have been Lucky or Kane, but they had dropped out of sight.

The song continued; he logged into his computer and read over everything Paul had told them about what he saw in the great battle. *Should I expand our search and battle?* He already knew the answer. Find the problem, find a solution, and fix the problem. It is what he had been doing for years.

After his mother was killed, he and his father traveled for a while. There was insurance money, and his father had a decent job as a traveling salesperson. They put everything they could away, and as it turned out, Tommy was excellent at figuring out patterns. They used knowledge and invested in the right stocks

# AFTERWORD

at the right time, which allowed them to fund this small group eventually.

Until now, they had not carried weapons. Who in the public would be upset by a group of people carrying only big flashlights? But that reality may have to change. *A flaming sword would be cool.*

They had come across some of them before. Never like this demon, but old stories of the giants and the Nephilim. He would tell his team to be on the lookout for other oddities.

Sarah lay on the dock, and Jeff and Angel were in the water. It had taken Jeff did a bit of coaxing to teach her to swim. The only investment they'd spent any money on was to add lots of sand. They turned one side of the lake into a small beach. They have never had a lot of friends, but those they had now were true friends, and while there was always the undercurrent of the mission, they were all dedicated to it.

There was also the need for downtime and to move forward with their lives. Sarah rubbed her belly. She hadn't told Jeff yet, but she would tell him tonight. Angel seemed to have been the first to know. *That dog is too smart,* Sarah thought to herself when Angel came over to the bed one morning, placed her head on her tummy, and looked up at her.

Jeff splashed around with the dog, laughed, and threw the frisbee toward the shore. It landed and floated on the water. Angel turned and, half swimming, half leaping, snatched the frisbee, then moved to shore. She ran to Sarah on the dock and dropped it at her feet. Now, Sarah was supposed to pick it up and throw it far so that she could race Jeff to it.

Angel had taught them this game once she realized she could stand in most of the lake before learning to swim. The trainer told Sarah that with Mastiffs, some take to the water, and some don't, so you have to see what they like. She and Jeff laughed heartily at his instruction and said, "Just treat her like she's human."

Sarah picked up the frisbee, and Angel prepared to launch

## AFTERWORD

herself into the water. Jeff was standing in the water, ready. He was feeling so good now.

He still worked out with Alex, but that was more for her than him. They had started martial arts training as well, and depending on what Sarah wanted to do, he figured they would help at the facility, whether physically or just with money. He would be happier helping in person but did not want Sarah to be worried.

Standing she looked at Jeff, Got ready to throw the frisbee, rubbed her belly and said, "We will call her Tina." Jeff's jaw dropped in surprise, and Sarah threw the frisbee.

Angel was off, and there was no chance for Jeff to catch up; he smiled at his wife and yelled back, "I love you!" then turned and dove into the water, trying to catch up to Angel for the frisbee.

# FROM THE AUTHOR

I'm David Musser, and this is my second novella. I hope you enjoyed this story based on the *Keep in the Light Universe*. When I write, I am not sure where the story will go. I admit I did hope at first to hear from Lucky and Kane again, and even Grandpa, but this is where the story went. I was happy to see what happened to Tommy and even the Man in White. His name is … now, what was it? I promise I will write it down.

Please visit dmusser.com for news. I do not know what the next story will be, but I promise you that I will do my best to make it entertaining for you.

I mentioned before that I find that music helps me concentrate when writing, and I have included my music list below, and for the record, I did have the song "Click Click Boom" by Saliva stuck in my head for a while during this.

Please feel free to let me know your thoughts on this book: <feedback@dmusser.com>

---

To learn more about David Musser and discover more Next Chapter authors, visit our website at www.nextchapter.pub.

## MUSIC PLAYLIST

When writing, I found that music helped me focus. I thought it would be good to include my playlist for anyone interested:

1. Ain't No Rest for the Wicked -- Cage the Elephant
2. Enter Sandman -- Metallica
3. Ghosts -- Sugarhouse
4. Black Hole Sun -- Soundgarden
5. Come As You Are -- Nirvana
6. Scar Tissue -- Red Hot Chili Peppers
7. Bad Girlfriend -- Theory Of A Deadman
8. I Hate Everything About You -- Three Days Grace
9. Smooth -- Santana \[feat. Rob Thomas\]
10. Baby One More Time -- Britney Spears
11. Click Click Boom -- Saliva

Whispers of Gray
ISBN: 978-4-82419-523-4

Published by
Next Chapter
2-5-6 SANNO
SANNO BRIDGE
143-0023 Ota-Ku, Tokyo
+818035793528

2nd July 2024

www.ingramcontent.com/pod-product-compliance
Lightning Source LLC
LaVergne TN
LVHW040106080526
838202LV00045B/3800